GHOUL DUTY

Sheriff Francis Hood Book Two

RICHARD F. MCGONEGAL

GHOUL DUTY

Sheriff Francis Hood Book Two

RICHARD F. MCGONEGAL

A Cave Hollow Press Book

Warrensburg, Missouri 2022

Cave Hollow Press™

Cave Hollow Press
304 Grover Street
Warrensburg, MO 64093

Copyright 2022 by Richard F. McGonegal
Formatting and cover design by Stephanie Flint
Cover Stock Images from DepositPhotos

Library of Congress Control Number: 2021948801

Paperback Edition ISBN-13: 978-1-7342678-1-5

Cave Hollow Press™

This book is dedicated to my wife Kristie, daughters Heather and Jane, and sister Carol for believing in me and inspiring me.

CHAPTER

1

Sheriff Francis Hood hated Ghoul Duty.

He scanned the flood-swollen Missouri River where light from the setting sun glistened on its muddy surface. A steady current slapped an almost hypnotic rhythm on the hull of the 14-foot johnboat as Hood and his chief deputy, Gus "Wally" Wallendorf, motored slowly upstream. The cloying humidity of the May evening settled on Hood as he sat stiffly in the bow of the boat. He brushed at a persistent gnat and exhaled a fraction of the tension he had brought aboard.

Even at its most benign, treachery lurked beneath the surface of the river. The menacing flood had prompted levee breaks, evacuations, and rescue efforts that occupied law enforcement agencies, including the Huhman County Sheriff's Department, for weeks. Adding proverbial insult to injury, floodwaters had inundated Our Lady of Help parish cemetery, disinterred 87 coffins, and carried the corpses downstream.

Hood wasn't certain where the phrase Ghoul Duty originated, although rumor held it was coined within his department. He didn't condone the moniker, but conceded it was an apt description for the collective duty to recover the remains. Although Hood dreaded the task—like any associated with a body of water—he participated, in keeping with his philosophy never to send deputies on assignments he wouldn't do himself. He had, however, purposely paired himself with Wally, who sat behind him in the stern and guided the craft. Wally had grown up along the river, respected both its power and unpredictability, and was the department's most skillful boat pilot.

Hood swiveled his head left to right in an attempt to relax the muscles in his neck and shoulders. The four-hour search had yielded nothing. Now that it was drawing to a close, he knew he should feel some professional disappointment about the unproductive search, but his only emotion was relief.

"What's that?" Wally asked, his voice disrupting the steady hum of the motor.

"Where?"

"There," Wally pointed. "In those branches off port."

Hood hesitated, evidence of his nautical ignorance.

"On the left," Wally clarified.

Hood squinted into the glare of diminishing sunlight and focused on an incongruous mass lodged in a fork of branches angling above the water. "Can't tell from here."

"Better check it out."

His deputy's deferential tone suggested Hood could overrule the recommendation, particularly in the waning daylight. The sheriff shifted in his seat and faced Wally, who wore an expectant expression.

"All right," Hood said. "Let's take a look." He faced forward and grimaced as Wally maneuvered the boat upstream in a sweeping semi-circle, then angled back downstream across the powerful current toward their target along the south bluff.

"Is it one?" Wally asked as they approached.

Hood was silent; he wasn't certain.

When they closed to within a few yards of the entanglement, both men had the answer. The stench was a foul combination of rotting flesh, decaying vegetation, and stagnant water. The corpse was wedged in a crook of branches, almost as if the river had spat it out. The left arm dangled limply in the water and seemed to beckon as the current tugged incessantly at its hand.

Wally killed the motor and allowed the boat to drift into the web of cottonwood limbs, then grabbed one of the stouter branches and steadied the craft. "What d'ya think?"

Hood stared at the body, thankful that a cluster of leaves shielded his view of the inanimate face. He lifted his powerful frame from the plank seat and braced his knees against the gunnel. The boat swayed. "If you can keep us still, I think I can haul him in," Hood said. His officious tone masked the ripples of queasiness in his gut.

"Okay," Wally said. He lashed a rope to a sturdy branch and pulled to remove the slack. "How's that?"

"Fine," Hood said, a monosyllabic response to the boat's stability, not the coming chore.

The sheriff turned his head and took a long breath. He braced his shins against the starboard hull, reached over the side, and clasped the corpse in a bear hug. He tried to visualize clutching a large, damp sack of grain, but the gelatinous bloat of the body was unmistakable.

Hood pulled. The branches swayed; the body didn't budge. He released his grasp, straightened, and exhaled audibly. "See if you can tug on the legs," he said. "They're stuck on something."

"Hold on." Wally wrapped the rope around a boat cleat, shifted position and reached for the corpse.

The boat rocked and Hood pitched forward. His arms flailed wildly and he grabbed onto a branch, narrowly averting a fall overboard. He glared at Wally.

"Sorry," Wally apologized. "I said, 'Hold on.'"

"I thought you meant hold on a second." Hood released the branch and steadied himself. "Never mind. Let me try again."

Wally sat back in the stern and pulled slack from the rope still attached to the boat cleat.

Hood sucked in another breath and wrapped his arms around the corpse's abdomen. He swallowed back the nausea now gathering into waves. He locked his wrists with his large hands, set his knees against the gunnel, and yanked violently.

A fitful moan shattered the evening stillness.

Hood tumbled backward into the boat's hull, smothered by body and branches.

"Tree's uprooted," Wally shouted as the powerful current caught the dislodged cottonwood tree and sent it careening downstream. Wally tore wildly at the wrappings around the cleat in a desperate attempt to free them but the last measure of slack tightened, spinning the johnboat and violently pitching it sideways.

Cold, muddy water poured over the side and swamped Hood as he fought to free himself from beneath the sodden bulk of the corpse. He craned his neck forward to prevent his face from being submerged, gasped for air, and inhaled the putrid scent of death.

Wally worked frantically to undo the windings, but the rope remained taut as the cottonwood towed the johnboat in its wake.

"Cut the rope," Hood shouted.

His deputy already was grappling to free his knife from its sheath. He clutched the rope, buried the blade in the braid, and sawed feverishly. The rope went slack, and Hood felt a rush of relief as the johnboat bobbed in the current, free of the cottonwood's tow. He wrestled himself out from under the corpse, then looked ahead and saw a newfound threat. The leafy silhouette of a stand of protruding treetops loomed in their path as the current carried the boat downstream.

Wally yanked the motor's starter cord once, twice. The outboard coughed, but failed to start. He pulled the cord again. Hood struggled to control his fear as he gauged the moments before the impending collision. He scrambled to his knees, saw the web of branches ahead, and shouted, "We're gonna hit."

Wally scowled. He adjusted the throttle and ripped at the starter cord. The motor belched and sputtered, then settled into a steady hum. He advanced the throttle and turned the craft sharply. Hood was tossed sideways. Branches raked his face, ripped his shirt and scraped along the hull as the johnboat shot through the periphery of a treetop and emerged into open water.

"You okay?" Wally yelled, as he regained control of the boat.

Hood turned to his deputy. The sheriff's face was a mask of blood and scratches, but his expression revealed a survivor's smile. Wally glanced at the corpse lying face down in the hull between them. "At least we got him," he said. Hood stared at the body and considered the irony of nearly getting themselves killed retrieving a corpse.

He really hated Ghoul Duty.

CHAPTER

2

Evenings were the worst.

Although Hood had been sober for more than nine months and his cravings had diminished, thoughts of drinking persisted. His shift on the river had left him physically drained, but emotionally charged.

Before he began his program of recovery, the end of a workday had marked the time for his first drink. He never drank in the morning because he reasoned if he could limit his drinking to evenings only, he must not be an alcoholic. His denial eroded over time. He began to suspect the profuse sweating he experienced every morning was a symptom of withdrawal. Although he tried desperately to cling to the illusion he remained in control, he knew—in his heart of hearts—the drinking had taken on a life of its own. Obsession and compulsion dictated his thoughts and behaviors. And, in time, alcoholism broke up his family; his wife, Linda, took their teenage daughter, Elizabeth, and left. For a time, they stayed with relatives. Eventually, they moved to a rental on the western edge of St. Gotthard, the county seat.

Hood remained in touch with his wife and daughter. Whenever Linda's extended family hosted a gathering, she invited him. About three times a month, depending on their schedules, the three of them would go out to dinner, and periodically Hood and Elizabeth would get together for some activity. He immediately had said yes when Linda asked if he could take their daughter to cheerleader tryouts the next day.

Matthew, Hood's sponsor in recovery, had promised at their first meeting, "If you stick with a program of recovery, your life will get better. It may not be everything you want— your family may not be reunited—but your life will be better." The promise had come true, partially. Hood knew he had changed. His attitude had improved. He had become more honest, tolerant, open to new ideas, and willing to adapt. Ultimately, however, he hoped his transformation would encourage his wife and daughter to come home. They hadn't, at least not yet, and each passing day depleted his hopes.

He had expected his loneliness also would diminish, but it had not.

This evening—like most evenings—he felt alone.

The emptiness in the house was palpable. It followed him from room to room, followed him into the kitchen, followed him past the now-empty liquor cabinet. He removed a water glass from an upper cabinet and filled it with crushed ice and chilled water from the dispenser on the refrigerator door. He carried the drink to the family room, briefly considering the irony of the term *family* room as he set the glass on a coaster. He kicked off his shoes, stretched out on the sofa, and used the TV remote to locate a Cardinals' baseball game.

GHOUL DUTY

His recovery program reminded him to be grateful for what he had, not resentful about what he lacked. The game was only in the third inning and the score was close. Small pleasures, he thought.

CHAPTER

3

A solid oak door emblazoned with a five-point star and black, block letters shadowed with gold identified the Huhman County Sheriff's Department. The offices were located in the basement of the stately limestone courthouse on the cusp of downtown St. Gotthard.

Hood cradled the nearly empty coffee container advertising At Your Convenience—a routine morning stop—as he swiped his security card and pushed open the door. He greeted some of the early day-shift arrivals and beelined to the coffee maker, located on a counter near the dispatcher's station.

As expected, his dependable dispatcher, Maggie O'Brien, was at her post. During Hood's 22-year tenure with the department—including the last nine as its leader—he could not recall an occasion when Maggie was absent or late on a scheduled workday. Maggie looked up and focused on the red crosshatch of welts scratched into her boss's right cheek and forehead. "Rough night?" she asked.

"Ghoul Duty." Hood filled the disposable cup with office coffee and replaced the plastic lid. He possessed a collection of ceramic cups, including a Boss's Day gift from Maggie, but rarely used one. All were stained or scattered around the office, abandoned whenever he had been abruptly called away.

"So I heard," she said.

Hood sipped coffee and stared quizzically at Maggie.

"Wally clued me in," she said.

"He's here?"

"Already at his desk when I got in."

"Why so early?"

Maggie shrugged. "Could ask you the same thing on your day off."

"Need to catch up on some reports. I promised my wife I'd take Elizabeth to cheerleader tryouts this afternoon," he said, referencing his daughter's ambition to make the team as a rising sophomore. He peered into Maggie's nearly empty cup—a large, novelty item that warned: Guess My Age and Win a Fat Lip. "More coffee?" he asked.

"I'll take a warmer."

As he poured, the switchboard rang and Maggie answered. He eavesdropped as she gathered information and assured the caller a deputy would respond. She disconnected, keyed numbers into the radio, and said, "Base to five-seven-four."

"This is five-seven-four," answered the familiar voice of Deputy Lester Stackhouse. "Go ahead base."

"We've got another report of mailbox baseball," Maggie said. Mailbox baseball referred to the growing pastime among teen vandals who would travel county roads and clobber mailboxes with a baseball bat. "Address is one-four-one-six Greystone Road. Complainant is Emma Schuelein."

"I'll add her to the list," Lester said. "Anything else?"

"All for now," Maggie said. She disconnected.

"Much happen overnight?" Hood asked.

"Other than mailbox baseball going into extra innings, not a lot. There was a two-vehicle wreck on Route AA, just this side of the county line, and an attempted burglary at the Route D Whoa 'N' Go." The switchboard phone rang. "Oh, and a domestic disturbance at Hickory Hills Estates."

"I guess the folks in the high-rent district have their problems, too."

"I guess." She lifted the receiver, covered the mouthpiece, and added, "Reports are on your desk, except the ones Lester's still working."

Hood headed for his office, but paused at the open doorway of Wally's office. "Morning," he greeted.

Wally sat amid a clutter of documents littering his desk, looked up from the one he had been reading, and winced at his boss's facial wounds.

Hood and Wally posed a study in contrasts that would delight a caricaturist. Hood was all bulk and curved lines. He carried about 210 pounds, mostly muscle, on a frame slightly short of six feet tall. His biceps, forearms, thighs, and calves were thick, his shoulders and chest broad, and his waist trim. His round head was topped with short, sandy-brown hair, and his face was dominated by a natural, almost perpetual, smile. He was conscious of the smile and, at times, worried it might undermine his ability to command or intimidate. Wally, however, was all sharp lines and angles. He was lanky, sinewy, and stood six feet, four inches tall. His face was almost gaunt, with narrow eyes, thin lips, and a tangle of unruly brown hair. Wally's uniform seemed to dangle from his skeletal body, whereas Hood's was well-fitted and worn with military precision.

"Morning," Wally mumbled.

"You're in early."

"Yeah."

Hood guessed from his chief deputy's tone and manner that he was blaming himself for the brush with disaster on the river. "For what it's worth," Hood said, "things worked out okay last night."

Wally stared at his desktop. "I nearly got us killed."

"Actually," Hood said, "the river nearly got us killed."

"I never should've tied up to that tree. I should've known better."

Hood waited silently for a few moments, then turned to leave and nearly collided with Maggie, who had approached and held out a sheet of paper.

"DOC just sent this over," she said, referring to the Missouri Department of Corrections.

"What's up?" Wally asked as his boss scanned the document.

"Just a reminder," Hood said. "Heath Schrock's being released today."

"Schrock," Wally repeated.

"This morning at ten," Maggie said, her tone betraying uneasiness.

"Let's all just take it easy," Hood said.

"Easy?" Wally said. "You remember what Schrock said to you?"

Hood remembered all too well. As Schrock was led away from the courtroom, he faced Hood and said, "Your time will come, Francis. Tick tock." Hood knew some wounds healed over time; others just festered. The nine years that had elapsed since Schrock's conviction was a long time, but Hood knew the wound he had inflicted was deep. "Let's not blow this out of proportion," he said. "Okay?"

He waited until both Wally and Maggie nodded agreement, then added, "I'll be in my office."

Hood dropped the DOC notice on top of the papers piled on his massive oak desk. The desk and the three mismatched captain's chairs facing it were antiquated, if not antiques—all handed down by Hood's predecessor, Sheriff Cliff Westerman.

Hood lowered himself into his chair—an oak swivel chair he had outfitted with a cushion—and picked up the copy of the morning newspaper Maggie customarily positioned on the corner of his desk.

The lead story covered a recurring subject—the flood. He read that the Missouri River was expected to set another record crest, another rural levee had been breached, and sandbagging efforts continued as Central Missourians "struggled valiantly" to protect their homes and properties. He flipped to the page where the article was continued and found a companion story updating efforts to recover the bodies disinterred from Our Lady of Help cemetery. The remains of Ned Diekroeger and Esther Willenbrink, both retrieved by the State Water Patrol, had been identified and released for reburial by Fredrickson Mortuary, one of two funeral homes assisting the process. Hood noted the news story omitted mention of the body he and Wally had delivered last night, and speculated the newspaper's deadline preceded identification of the corpse.

He set the newspaper aside, shuffled through the reports and stopped when the name Cheryl Grimm grabbed his attention. The nature of the report was a domestic disturbance, and the responding officer was Young John, his rookie deputy. An involuntary shudder radiated along Hood's spine as he read:

Narrative of Deputy John Bunch

At 7:46 p.m. on Tuesday, May 18, I responded to a report of a disturbance at a private residence at 1406 Manor Court in the Hickory Hills Estates in western Huhman County. On arrival, I observed a man and a woman shouting at each other in the front yard. I observed a front window had been broken, and the front door was open. I approached the couple, stepped between them, and advised them I was responding to a reported disturbance. The man identified himself as David Grimm and the woman as his wife Cheryl. Neither was injured and the husband was immediately apologetic. He claimed a routine argument had gotten out of hand. He confessed he had thrown a paperweight and broken a window, and when his wife left through the front door, he had followed her outside and continued the argument.

I talked privately with Cheryl, who was satisfied the argument was over. She requested no further action.

I warned the couple to stop the argument and go back inside. I also explained that if authorities were dispatched again, state law would require us to arrest one or both of the parties involved.

I left the premises at approximately 8 p.m.

Hood dropped the report on his desk. Memories flooded his mind. Cheryl Grimm, whose maiden name was Verslues, had been Hood's childhood sweetheart. They had lived in the same neighborhood as children, were elementary school classmates, and began dating in high school. He always had felt she was—what was the phrase they used back then?—out of his league, so his infatuation was coupled with a feeling of pride when they were seen together in public. Hood vividly remembered the euphoria he felt from basking in the envious looks of his peers whenever he escorted Cheryl to high school activities in his restored 1970 Chevelle SS.

And he never forgot the humiliating episode in his junior year when David Grimm pushed him to the ground and—in one brief moment—changed everything.

Hood still thought about Cheryl on occasion, particularly when he saw her face on a billboard or her name in the newspaper's real estate section. Professionally, she had retained her maiden name, Verslues, because it was a respected, longtime Huhman County surname, in contrast to the less familiar name of her husband, an Illinois native.

Hood's desk phone rang, flushing his musings like a bevy of quail. He lifted the receiver. "I have a call for you from a Mrs. Sandbothe at Our Lady of Help Catholic Church," Maggie said.

"Put her through." Hood awaited the transfer, then said, "This is your sheriff."

"Good morning, Sheriff," a pleasant, but officious, voice greeted. "This is Nettie Sandbothe, the secretary at Our Lady of Help and director of the cemetery association."

"Good morning," Hood said.

"I'm calling about the body you brought to Fredrickson Mortuary last night. I just had a conversation with Mr. Fredrickson, the funeral director."

"Yes," Hood said, his tone bright with anticipation of her appreciation.

"I'm afraid he isn't one of ours."

The words hit like a punch in the gut. Although he had heard them clearly, he was confounded. He gathered himself. "What do you mean he isn't yours?"

"Exactly that. The body Mr. Fredrickson examined doesn't match anyone in our cemetery records. I've checked and double-checked. They're quite comprehensive. Mr. Fredrickson also said—"

"You're sure?" Hood interrupted, although he knew from her tone she was.

"Quite sure."

"Then who is he?" Hood blurted, awash in confusion.

"I haven't the foggiest. Mr. Fredrickson said—"

"Could there be some records that are lost, or misplaced?"

"Sheriff," Mrs. Sandbothe said, her voice polite, but firm, "as I was about to tell you, Mr. Fredrickson agrees wholeheartedly, based on his examination. He said—"

"But how could a funeral director know if records are missing?"

"Sheriff," Mrs. Sandbothe said, "Mr. Fredrickson said the body you brought in was never embalmed."

CHAPTER

4

"Flitex, blitex, mitex," Heath Schrock muttered as he walked along the sidewalk bordering Hart Street. He stopped in front of a law office and looked across the street at the entrance to the Huhman County Courthouse. The limestone building dominated a corner of the downtown, a mix of dedicated third-generation retailers, eateries, artsy specialty shops, and empty storefronts. The second stories and side streets were occupied mostly by attorneys, who had established offices in close proximity to the judiciary. The namesake of the county was Col. Stephen Huhman, who had commanded a frontier fort to protect what was then a thriving rail and steamboat hub along the Missouri River.

"Mukes, blukes, kalukes," Schrock mumbled as he scanned the courthouse parking lot and focused on the sheriff's department vehicles — newer four-wheel-drive SUVs and cruisers including Dodge Chargers and a few Ford Crown Victorias. Schrock removed the "gently worn" jacket of his prison-issued, powder-blue suit and dangled it over his shoulder.

A magician might describe Schrock's appearance as illusory — something that is not what it seems. His pale complexion, rust-red curly hair, and the galaxy of freckles that bridged his nose and sprinkled his cheeks suggested softness. His oversized shirt hid the muscled definition of his upper body. Although he was not a big man, comparatively, he had developed the quick reflexes, fighting prowess, and situational awareness needed to survive nine years of living among brutes.

As he propped the sole of his shoe against the building's brick facade, a man with a cigarette perched between his lips stepped outside of the law office and stood beside him. The man lit the cigarette as he glanced at Schrock.

Schrock stared at him.

"No smoking in the building," the man explained, as if in answer to a question.

"Give you two bucks for a smoke," Schrock said.

The man assessed Schrock, then took a pack from his shirt pocket and, with a practiced tap, produced a protruding cigarette. "Take one," he said. "No charge."

"I look like some kind of charity case to you?" Schrock dropped the suit jacket on the sidewalk, pulled a tangle of bills from his pocket and peeled off two singles.

"You can buy a whole pack for five bucks," the man said.

Schrock plucked a cigarette from the pack and put it between his lips. "If I wanted a pack, I'd buy a fuckin' pack." He shoved the singles in the man's shirt pocket.

"Look, I was just trying to be—"

"Don't push it," Schrock said.

The man flicked his cigarette into the street, muttered "whatever" and disappeared back inside the building.

GHOUL DUTY

* * * * *

Hood pressed the doorbell.

Linda, dressed in her nurse's uniform, opened the door almost immediately. "Elizabeth," she called into the emptiness behind her. "Your father's here to take you to cheerleading tryouts."

"Coming," a disembodied voice shouted.

"Come on in," Linda said to her husband. "Thanks for doing this," she added as he entered the front room.

Hood almost said, *She's my daughter, too,* but didn't. Although she always had been his daughter, not so long ago—when he was drinking—he hadn't been much of a father. When drunk, Linda never asked him to drive Elizabeth; when sober, he balked at being inconvenienced. "Glad I could help," he said.

Linda stood on her tiptoes and kissed his cheek. "Got to run," she said. She left, and Hood felt any movement toward reconciliation leave with her. Months ago, he had stopped reminding her she and Elizabeth could come home any time. He had stopped asking her when she might be ready. He had followed the advice of Matthew, his sponsor in recovery, who suggested patience, not pleadings.

"Hi, daddy," Elizabeth said, as she emerged into the hallway.

Hood was unable to mask his surprise. Although he had continued to interact with his daughter during the separation, she typically wore an oversized t-shirt, baggy shorts, and little

21

makeup. The gangly adolescent daughter who now stood before him had transformed herself into a young woman. Her facial features were accentuated by impeccable makeup, her dusty blonde hair was styled in a long ponytail, and she wore a form-fitting sweater and what Hood considered a profoundly short skirt.

"Hi," Hood said.

They left the house, buckled their seatbelts, and sat silently during the drive until Hood asked, "So, how many girls do you think will be trying out?"

"Dunno."

"Is it a large squad? I mean, how many girls are in it?"

"Dunno," she repeated.

"Is Claire trying out?" he persisted, referencing his daughter's best friend.

"Yeah. Her mom's bringing her. I told her I'd meet her there."

His hope for quality father-daughter time diminished. He gave up his questioning and yielded to the quiet. Elizabeth seemed sullen, prompting Hood to wonder if her mood was a continuing consequence of his alcoholism. Matthew had warned him to avoid assumptions. Blaming yourself for everyone else's mood or problem is just another form of ego, Matthew had said. You don't have that much influence over people. Sometimes, people just have a bad day. The reminder brought a measure of solace, which lasted until he parked in the Huhman County R-1 High School lot and switched off the ignition.

Elizabeth immediately hopped out, said "Thanks," and shut the door.

Hood watched as his daughter and the other girls seated themselves in the outdoor bleachers and listened while the squad's co-captains—identified by the gold C's embroidered on their uniforms—shouted instructions interspersed with demonstrations of established routines. It wouldn't take a detective, he thought, to observe the superior attitudes in the way they stepped, pivoted, and cheered in unison.

His thoughts meandered from the body in the river, to Heath Schrock's release, to the domestic violence incident involving his high school sweetheart. *Be here*, he reminded himself, a phrase he had borrowed from a member of his recovery group, who often repeated the axiom: "Wherever you are, be there."

What he wanted, however, was to be somewhere else. He watched his daughter watch the upper-class girls who would decide her fate as a cheerleader, as if that mattered. But it did matter. He remembered his own experiences in high school—striving to be popular, or at least to fit in. He had enjoyed popularity, but also had experienced humiliation. He remembered the day David Grimm knocked him down. The physical wounds were slight, but the mental and emotional damage left a resentment akin to scar tissue. He wondered how his daughter would react if she didn't make the team. Would she be devastated? He tried to imagine himself in her situation, in her world.

The bleachers began to empty, igniting his hopes that the

tryouts were over. Instead, the under-class girls were taking the field to demonstrate their abilities.

Elizabeth ran to his cruiser. "I'm going to catch a ride home with Claire and her mom," she said.

"You sure? I can stay."

"It could be a while. It's fine." Elizabeth glanced toward the field and focused on the seeming glare of disapproval from one of the co-captains. "I gotta go."

"Okay." Hood knew a dismissal when he heard one. He started the ignition.

As afternoon yielded to early evening, Heath Schrock stood on a concrete slab and rapped on the front door of a small, sad-looking house in rural Huhman County. While he waited, he scanned the mold-stained vinyl siding that was separating at the corners. A gutter hung askew, detached from its downspout, and scattered clumps of weeds protruded from a muddy front yard.

"Who is it?" a voice called.

"That you, Ronnie? It's me, Heath."

Ronnie pulled the door open. He hesitated momentarily, as if appraising his cousin, then stepped forward and hugged him. "Wow, man, you grew up. How long's it been?"

"Nine years."

"Nine fucking years," Ronnie said. He disengaged from the hug and stood silently in place, as if unsure of what to say or do next.

"You get my message?" Heath asked.

"Yeah, sure, but those guys you sent here didn't say when you were getting out exactly."

A brief, awkward silence followed before Heath said, "Well, I'm out now."

"Yeah, yeah. C'mon in. Make yourself at home."

Heath followed Ronnie into the living room and was nearly overpowered by the odor of marijuana. "Shit, Ronnie, this place reeks."

"Yeah. Sorry, man. That's my roommate Freddie. He's not here right now. Probably out peddling product. Have a seat. Want a beer?"

"Sure," Heath said. He settled into a sagging couch that cushioned him only marginally better than sitting on the floor.

"Freddie's a stoner, but he's a fucking ATM, man," Ronnie said, as he opened the refrigerator. "Keeps us in rent, groceries, and plenty of smoke, snort, sniff, whiff, even a little shot in the arm if you're inclined." He returned to the living room and handed his cousin a beer.

"You get my stuff taken care of?" Heath asked.

"Yeah, sure. By the way, those guys who came here were some mean-ass mothers."

"Sorry about that," Heath said. "I didn't send 'em. Friend of mine on the inside did me a favor. He's pretty well connected—better to have as a friend than an enemy. His guys didn't rough you up or anything?"

"No, no. But they scared the fuck out of us. I thought Freddie was gonna shit a brick of weed."

"So it's okay if I hang here a while?"

"Okay with me. Freddie's a little, you know, but he's paranoid about everything. He's worried you'll give Probation and Parole this address."

"Already did," Heath said, "but there's no reason for them to come around unless I miss my appointments." He surveyed the interior surroundings. "Is Freddie gonna be a problem?"

Ronnie gauged the displeasure evident in his cousin's expression. "No," he said, his tone assuring. "It's cool. He'll come around."

"Good," Heath said. "What about my dad's old truck?"

"Yeah. I went to your old place—it's falling apart, by the way—and got the truck running. I didn't get it registered or anything. I didn't know what you wanted. It's around back."

"Good," Heath said. "And the sheriff?"

"You mean that stakeout shit? Yeah, I wrote it all down—where he goes, what he does when." Ronnie rummaged through a heap of papers, fast-food containers, and drug paraphernalia atop a wooden coffee table. He located a notepad and passed it to Heath. "You know, I don't mean to be sticking my nose in—" he began, stopping himself in mid-sentence when Heath looked from the pad to his cousin.

"What?"

Ronnie shrugged. "I don't know. I figure something's on your mind. I know you guys have history, but you just got out of the joint and he's, like, the fucking sheriff, man. I mean, if your plan—"

Heath's laughter was so deep and sudden, it startled his cousin. "Ronnie, I don't have a plan. It's not like I sat in prison for nine years cooking up some plan. I just take life as it comes." He swigged beer. "But he did what he did and now he's the fucking sheriff, and I'm free, and—" he shrugged, "we'll see."

"I just don't want you to end up back in prison," Ronnie said. "I mean, it's not like your old man was ever—"

"Don't," Heath said, a warning note in his tone. "I know what he was, but he was still my father. There's gotta be some payback." He tipped the beer to his lips and took a long, satisfying swallow.

CHAPTER
5

Hood entered the aptly named convenience store, At Your Convenience, and walked to the familiar self-serve coffee bar.

Years had passed—six, perhaps seven—since Curt Rackers had retired as the longtime operator of the full-service Sinclair station and sold the property at the coveted corner to the convenience store chain.

Hood sipped the steaming liquid cautiously as he approached the counter, paid the cashier, and exited.

Once outside, he took another sip and looked up. His shoulders convulsed with a sudden spasm and coffee sloshed onto his fingers. "Son of a bitch," he mumbled as he stared at the battered, black pickup truck, a Chevy half-ton. The sight of the tortured truck triggered a memory from nine years ago when Curt owned the station and Hood served as chief deputy to his boss and mentor, Sheriff Cliff Westerman.

Hood had gone inside to buy two coffees from the vending machine in Curt's cluttered office/waiting area while Westerman checked the air pressure in the cruiser's tires.

Westerman had served two decades as county sheriff and seemed to be on a first-name basis with everyone within his jurisdiction. He was revered or reviled, depending on which side of the law a person stood. Hood considered Westerman tough, fair, and smart — smart enough to realize he was among an endangered species of lawmen. His limited education left him befuddled by the technology that was beginning to infiltrate his department. And he readily admitted he was more comfortable confronting an armed felon than computer software.

Westerman possessed an uncanny instinct about how people would react to circumstances, a talent Hood had attempted to absorb during the time they worked together. Hood had seen those instincts fail only once — on that morning years ago as he set the coffee cups on the counter to cool and chatted with Curt.

"So," Curt had asked, "how's Linda and that beautiful daughter?"

"Great," Hood said. He pulled a photograph from his uniform pocket. "That's from Elizabeth's birthday party."

Curt admired the photograph. "Kids are pretty special," he said. "I've got another grandbaby due this fall. That'll make five."

"Congratulations," Hood said. When their conversation concluded and he stepped outside, Westerman was not by the cruiser. Hood surveyed the property and saw his boss leaning into the passenger side of a black Chevy pickup parked on the far side of the lot.

The two popping sounds — one, then another in quick succession — momentarily confused him. He stood transfixed and immobilized. Then his mind registered the seeming unreality as he watched Westerman stagger backward and drop to one knee.

The pickup sped away.

Hood dropped the coffee cups and ran to Westerman. He lowered his boss to the pavement as blood gushed from two wounds — one in the shoulder and another in the gut. Blood stained the sheriff's uniform and warmed Hood's fingers as he applied pressure to the wounds.

"I'm all right, Francis," Westerman said, with typical bravado. "Call me an ambulance and go arrest that son of a bitch."

Curt came running across the lot, stopped when Hood shouted for him to call 9-1-1, then sprinted back to the station.

"I can't believe it," Westerman said. "I just went over to talk to him. See how he was doing on probation."

"Who?" Hood asked.

"Bobby Schrock."

"Schrock shot you?"

"Not him. His kid."

"Little Heath?"

"Ain't so little anymore."

"Just stay quiet," Hood said. In the silence that followed, he heard the keening siren of the approaching ambulance.

* * * * *

Hood's inquiry at the convenience store about the battered pickup yielded nothing. The clerk who typically rang up his morning coffee was not on duty, and her teen replacement lacked interest. "I don't even know if that's part of our lot," he had answered. None of the other customers claimed the truck, which had no license plates. Hood vacillated between leaving and waiting to see if the driver returned. He was curious about whether the black pickup was the same truck driven by Bobby Schrock nine years earlier or simply was a similar make and model. The vehicle's coincidental appearance and its lack of license plates, however, were creepy.

Hood checked his watch. He had a morning appointment with Loeffelman, the county medical examiner, and he didn't want to be late after he had cajoled the man into sacrificing part of his weekend to conduct an autopsy. Still, he made a visual inspection of the pickup—the cab was locked and no tools or personal possessions were evident—before yielding to his habit of punctuality and his eagerness to hear what Loeffelman had learned.

Hood arrived at the appointed time and was escorted to a spacious room designed for postmortem examinations and storage. Loeffelman was seated at a metal desk, listening to a recorder and jotting notes on a legal pad. "Morning," he greeted, without looking up. He motioned Hood to one of the chairs facing the desk. Hood sat, sipped coffee, and studied the man across from him.

A cubist might fret that a portrait of Loeffelman would seem more realistic than abstract. The medical examiner's face was rectangular and his jaw square. His dark eyes were accentuated with bushy black eyebrows, and his head was topped with curly, black hair highlighted with wisps of silver. Hood was among the Huhman County officials who appreciated the professional stature Loeffelman brought to their county government. Based on his expertise and experience, he frequently was sought for consultations and presentations by his peers not only in Missouri, but throughout the Midwest.

Loeffelman switched off the recorder, looked up, and examined the scratches on the sheriff's face. "Dare I ask?"

"Ghoul Duty," Hood said. He pointed to his cheek. "Got scratched up bringing in the guy I asked you to look at."

"You seemed in a bit of a rush when you called."

"Sorry," Hood said. "It's just that I've got nowhere to start until I know something—who this guy is, how he died, how long he's been dead, anything you can tell me."

"Well," Loeffelman said, "I don't have much in the way of answers, yet." He opened a manila folder on his desk and consulted a computer printout. "Remember, these are preliminary findings, but here's what we know. Your corpse is a white male, age approximately mid-30s, height five feet, ten inches, weight I'm guessing about 180, brown hair and brown eyes." Loeffelman looked up. "That's the easy part. There's substantial decomposition, so fingerprints won't help. Dental records are our best bet for identification. I've already sent those in. If that doesn't work, we'll try x-rays."

"How'd he die?"

"Blunt trauma to the head," Loeffelman said. Hood

noticed the medical examiner's tone gradually became more serious and more professional as he described the autopsy results. "He's got cranial damage sufficient to cause death. Could be homicide, could be an accident."

"Accident?"

"Tree limb could have fallen on his head — something like that. Of course, it's more likely someone whacked him with something — something solid, like a rock or baseball bat."

"He didn't drown?"

"No."

Hood swallowed a sip of coffee. "No water in the lungs?"

"You watch too much television, Francis," Loeffelman said. "Drowning isn't always consistent with heavy lungs." He observed the sheriff's puzzled expression and continued. "If you suck fresh water into your lungs and drown, after a while the water will transfer to the blood by osmosis because blood is saltier. So a drowning victim won't necessarily have water in the lungs. Drowning in salt water's a different story, but we're a long way from an ocean."

"How long?"

"About a thousand miles."

Hood smiled. "No, I mean how long's he been dead?"

Loeffelman leaned back and shrugged. "Hard to pinpoint. At least three weeks, not more than six. Standard indicators — stiffening, settling of blood, body temperature, stomach contents — all go out the window after that long. Plus, we've got some inconsistencies that are baffling as hell."

"Such as?"

"Well, for starters, he's got significant decomposition, which indicates weeks rather than days. But the condition of the body isn't consistent with being in a river that long. A corpse in the water that long is going to have more bloat, more discoloration."

"So where's he been?"

"Good question. As you know, the rate of decomposition corresponds to conditions. If a body's been in a cool, dry place, it will decompose more slowly than if it's been exposed to warmer temperatures and moisture. This spring has been hot, humid, and rainy, but this corpse hasn't been exposed to those conditions for as long as he's been dead."

Hood twisted his expression into a frown. "Are you saying someone stashed the body somewhere, then later on dumped it in the river?"

"What I'm saying is science tells me this body hasn't been in the river for three to six weeks. Not even close."

Hood pondered the questions Loeffelman had raised. If the body hadn't been in the river since death occurred, was it located indoors or outdoors? Could it have been in one of the houses, farm sheds, or other outbuildings swept away by more recent flooding? When did the man disappear? Who was the last person to see him? And who the hell was he?

"You're not giving me much to go on," Hood said.

"Sorry, Francis," Loeffelman said. "The dead sometimes answer questions, but sometimes they just add to the riddle."

CHAPTER
6

Ansel Creighorn's name was not on the ownership papers of The Sportsmen's Bar and Grill, but the staff and regular patrons both understood who ran the place. And when Creighorn's key ring—with its distinctive metal skull fob—was on the rail of the pool table, that was a signal other players were welcome only at his invitation.

Creighorn would be an ideal model for a fairy-tale illustrator seeking to draw a malevolent giant. Standing six-feet, four-inches tall and weighing more than 300 pounds, with dark, deeply set eyes framed by bushy black hair and a thick beard, intimidating newcomers rarely was a challenge for Creighorn. Customers who cowered were allowed to stay; anyone foolish enough to protest was beaten.

Lisa Monroe, the barmaid on duty, watched the stranger as he paused just inside the entrance and surveyed the evening crowd scattered amid the sprawling interior. She continued watching him as he crossed the width of the room and perched on a stool at the end of the long bar.

"What can I getcha?" she asked.

"Beer."

"We've got Bud, Bud Light—"

"Doesn't matter."

"Draft or bottle?"

"Doesn't matter either. Draft's good."

Lisa hesitated momentarily and looked beyond the stranger to the adjoining pool room, where Creighorn was preoccupied in a game with two of his cronies—Neil Bowden and Herman Wallendorf, the chief deputy's younger brother.

The stranger followed her lead and noted her focus on the big man.

"You may want to move down a stool or two," she advised.

"I'm fine here."

"Suit yourself," she said. She tapped the beer and set it before him. "That'll be $2.50."

He sipped the beer and gazed at her. The photograph he had been shown was an inferior image of the woman. A sculptor might be captivated by the challenge of reproducing her slender, but shapely, torso. Long dark hair framed facial features that expressed insouciance, but not sophistication. As he withdrew bills from his pocket and handed her a five, he said, "You're Lisa, right?"

"Who's asking?"

"Friend of Buddy's."

"You know Buddy?" Her tone thawed immediately with anticipation of news about her incarcerated husband.

"Shared a cell for a while." He extended his hand. "Name's Heath."

"He okay?" she asked as she shook his hand. "He says he is, but I—" She stopped in mid-sentence as Creighorn approached from the poolroom. He held an empty pitcher in one hand and a pool cue in the other.

"He's okay," Schrock said. "He's pretty good about keeping his nose out—"

His response was interrupted by the loud, abrupt slap of the empty pitcher on the counter. "Need a refill," Creighorn said. He turned to the stranger at the bar and glowered menacingly.

"Coming right up, Ansel," Lisa said.

As she hustled to refill the pitcher, Creighorn barked, "Shake it, Lisa. Got a game in progress."

"No manners," Schrock whispered audibly. He shook his head slightly as he looked with amused annoyance at Creighorn.

"And who the fuck are you?" Creighorn asked. He moved forward until his face was inches from the other man.

Lisa returned with the pitcher. "We don't need any trouble tonight, Ansel."

"Ain't gonna be no trouble if this asshole gets off my barstool."

Schrock sipped his beer. "Actually, my ass is pretty comfortable right where it is."

Without further warning, Creighorn raised the pool cue to strike, but Schrock already was in motion. He grabbed Creighorn's wrist, twisted the giant's arm, and kicked his feet out from under him. Creighorn toppled and hit the floor— hard. The point of his nose and chin bounced off the hardwood as the pool cue clattered beside him. Bar patrons turned to the commotion as Schrock scrambled astride the small of Creighorn's back and wrenched his left arm into a grotesque angle.

"Enough?" Schrock asked.

Creighorn unleashed a tirade of threats and curses, spitting, and spewing blood from his nose and mouth onto the floorboards. Schrock yanked Creighorn's arm, producing a dull pop as the limb dislocated from the shoulder socket, followed almost simultaneously by Creighorn's anguished howl.

"Enough?" Schrock repeated.

Creighorn lifted his head slightly and nodded.

Schrock arose and stepped back.

Creighorn clambered to his knees, held his dislocated arm, and grimaced in pain. He stared at the collective expressions of disbelief among the onlookers who had witnessed his defeat. He turned to face the man who had left him injured, bloodied, and humiliated, then hurried out the door. Schrock followed him to the door and peered through the single pane of glass. He watched from the interior as Creighorn crossed the gravel parking lot, approached a white pickup truck and opened the driver's door, which advertised Creighorn Excavating Co. in black block letters. Creighorn lifted a shotgun from the rack in the cab's rear window and started back toward The Sportsmen's.

When the door flew open moments later, everyone hit the floor except Schrock, who walloped Creighorn's good arm with a powerful upward sweep. The shotgun discharged, and plaster rained from the ceiling.

GHOUL DUTY

* * * * *

The buzz of conversation and speculation lingered among customers of The Sportsmen's after the altercation.

Schrock, heeding Lisa's advice, disappeared before the authorities responded.

An ambulance was first on the scene. The EMTs treated and transported Creighorn, but not before Herman Wallendorf retrieved Creighorn's key ring from the pool rail and returned it to the big man.

After the ambulance left, the murmurs resumed and amplified.

"Who was that guy?" one customer asked.

"Man, did you see what he did to Ansel?" another added.

"Never saw nobody put Ansel down like that," said a third.

"The guy looked familiar to me," said Neil Bowden, one of Creighorn's cronies. His comment attracted the curiosity of customers. "I know him from somewhere, but I can't place him."

"Can't swear to it," Herman said, "but I think that might be Bobby Schrock's kid."

Attention shifted to Herman, followed by a patron's remark: "I thought he was doin' time."

Herman shrugged. "Me too."

"Herman, what was that kid's name anyway?" someone asked.

"Heath, I think," Bowden said, seeking to regain the spotlight.

"Wasn't he that kid who shot old Sheriff Westerman?" another customer asked.

"Hey, Herman, wasn't your brother Wally in on that whole shootout afterward?"

"See, that's how shit gets started around here," Herman said, his anger and indignation apparent. "My brother never shot nobody."

The arrival of veteran sheriff's deputy Art Koeningsfeld quieted the conversation. Herman approached the officer and asked if his big brother was on duty. Told his older sibling had been delayed but was on his way, Herman thanked the deputy, rejoined the crowd momentarily, and slipped out the back door.

After last call and completion of her closing chores, Lisa left The Sportsmen's, accompanied by its owner Bill "Shep" Scheperle. Shep routinely escorted his female employees to their vehicles after the 1:30 a.m. closing. His presence was comforting, not because he was a formidable-looking companion, but because he carried a 9 mm handgun holstered beneath the brown suede vest he wore regularly.

When the incident occurred, Shep had been in the basement sorting crates from an afternoon delivery. The gunshot had brought him up the stairs, but not before Schrock had gone. Consequently, the man who stood beside a battered, black pickup at the far end of the parking lot was familiar to Lisa, but not to Shep.

"It's okay," Lisa said. She put a hand on Shep's shoulder to stop him from reaching inside his vest. "I know him."

"What's he doin' hangin' around here?" Shep asked.

"I think he wants to talk to me. You go on. I'll be fine."

"You sure?"

"Sure," she said, although she wasn't. "It's fine."

Shep hesitated, then walked to his truck. He lingered a moment while he watched Lisa and the stranger approach each other. He climbed into the cab but didn't start the engine.

"That the owner?" Schrock asked Lisa.

She nodded.

"Hope I didn't get you in trouble."

She shook her head. "Ansel's a regular, so trouble's regular. Usually it doesn't end with him in an ambulance—or a shotgun blast, for that matter."

Schrock shrugged.

The sound of an engine starting caused Lisa to look back at Shep's truck, which was idling but remained motionless. "Shep wanted to know why you're hanging around."

"I was just wondering if maybe you wanted to get a cup of coffee or something."

"Can't. I've got a kid," Lisa said, referencing her son, who was being watched by her mother-in-law while Lisa worked. "Gotta pick him up."

"Yeah. Buddy told me. Name's Cody, Corey, something like that."

"Cody." Lisa swung her long hair away from her eyes. The stranger, who had seemed so dominant and confident in the confrontation with Creighorn, now seemed somehow awkward and vulnerable. "You just get out—of prison, I mean?"

"Yesterday."

"You got a place to stay?"

"Yeah."

Lisa wasn't sure if he was telling the truth, but was glad he hadn't made some crude comment about whether she was offering her place. "What did you say your last name was?"

"I didn't, but it's Schrock. Heath Schrock. Ring a bell?

"No. Should it?"

"Some people remember."

"Remember what?"

"Me. Why I did time."

"Why did you do time?"

"Long story, but it's late and you got a kid to pick up." He paused. "Maybe another time. Good to meet you." He turned and walked to his truck.

Within minutes, the three vehicles remaining in the lot moved almost simultaneously and lined up as they left, each headed a separate way.

CHAPTER

7

Hood backed out of the garage and set his windshield wipers to correspond with the pace of the deluge of fat raindrops. He drove directly to At Your Convenience for his morning coffee, but he also was curious about whether the black truck was still parked there.

It wasn't.

Hood ran through the rain, greeted the regular cashier Harlene, and began his routine at the coffee bar. "Harlene," he said as he approached the register, "have you ever seen a pickup truck parked in that corner of the lot?" He gestured toward the spot. "Black, no plates, kinda beat up?"

"Can't say I have."

Hood paid and left. Inside the cruiser, he placed the cup in a holder and called the department. When Maggie answered, he told her he would be late because he planned to check on the Clarke Junction Levee.

She hesitated a beat, then asked, "You taking Old Sawmill Road?"

"Yeah."

"You want me to send someone? Lester's patrolling on the east side."

"No." He realized she already had made the connection;

the route would take him near Schrock's old house, or what was left of it. He sensed tension in the ensuing silence. "See you in an hour or so," he added, hoping to allay her concerns.

"Okay."

Hood disconnected, followed a familiar route, and turned onto the narrow Old Sawmill Road, which — true to its name — led to a now defunct sawmill on the banks of Clarke's Creek, a tributary of the Missouri River. He squinted through the windshield as sheets of rain created a funhouse-mirror effect — twisting and warping his view of hedgerows, trees, and fences. The road bisected sodden fields and edged upward to a knoll where a trio of faded mailboxes stood sentry beside an unmarked perpendicular lane. The lane's steep upward incline served three widely dispersed properties, including the Schrock place.

Hood ignored the turnoff and continued along Old Sawmill Road, following its descent about a mile until the remains of the abandoned mill appeared. Time had reduced the sawmill to a wizened, vanishing skeleton — a ghost conjured only by its namesake road. He eased to a stop and rolled down his driver's-side window to get a clearer view of the earthen embankment. The flood-swollen river had backed itself on the levee's bank, but the structure seemed solid.

The levee district that had built and maintained the bulwark was controlled almost exclusively by farmers, who had designed it to protect the fertile bottomlands that produced the crops vital to their livelihoods. The patchwork of corn and soybean fields was muddy from recent rainfall, but not flooded, accessed by what was little more than a rutted trail. It was used primarily during the planting and harvest seasons when Old Sawmill Road became a busy thoroughfare for tractors, reapers, and wagons that moved to and from the fields to higher ground. The trail also accessed a wooded area sprinkled with several rustic cabins originally built for seasonal use by hunters, although some had been abandoned and others were occupied year-round.

Those residents had been advised to evacuate until floodwaters receded; if the levee was breached, the devastation would be absolute. Still, a few of them resisted, including Ansel Creighorn, who had taken refuge in a cabin he upgraded after separating from a woman Hood believed was his second wife, but may have been his third.

Hood made a K-turn, backtracked along Old Sawmill Road, and without hesitation turned onto the muddy lane leading to the Schrock dwelling. He tried to recall how many years had elapsed since he had been to the dilapidated shack once inhabited by Bobby Schrock and his son. He recalled visiting one time in the past nine years, motivated solely by his curiosity about whether the structure still stood.

As he emerged from a natural canopy of treetops, the Schrock homestead began to emerge. The hovel was a ragged remainder, and reminder, of what it had been nearly a decade ago.

Nine years had elapsed, Hood remembered, since the day he had slid his boss's cruiser to a halt in the junk-

strewn yard as a shotgun blast shattered the vehicle's grille and headlights. After emergency medical personnel had loaded Sheriff Westerman into an ambulance and sped to the hospital, Hood had commandeered Westerman's cruiser, called for backup, and followed his boss's instruction to "go arrest that son of a bitch."

Wally, trailing in a second cruiser, skidded to a stop beside him, and Hood watched in horror as Bobby Schrock, standing on the shack's front porch, prepared to fire a second round. Hood saw his fellow deputy duck down in the moment before the shotgun blast disintegrated the windshield. Ripping his own 12-gauge shotgun from the dashboard rack, Hood shoved open the door and rolled onto the grass, returning fire from a prone position. His first blast snapped a porch support, and a portion of the shingled overhang swung down and careened into Bobby's shoulder. He staggered sideways but failed to go down. In that instant, Hood scrambled to his feet, pumped another shell into the chamber, and shouted for Bobby to drop his weapon.

He didn't.

Hood saw the wild, desperate look in the man's eyes. As Bobby swung the shotgun barrel toward him, Hood realized he had no alternative. He fired. The blast tore open Bobby's chest and splayed him against the door. He slumped slowly to the porch floor, leaving a broad smear of blood along the length of the peeling white paint on the door. The sheriff glanced back at the second cruiser and watched Wally emerge from the driver's door.

GHOUL DUTY

Hood chambered another round as he rushed to the porch, climbed the stairs, and without breaking stride, kicked the weapon from Bobby's lifeless hand. He slammed his shoulder into the front door and, as it flew open against its hinges, focused on where Heath might be, and whether he was armed. Hood filtered out the sounds of Wally scrambling to assist and concentrated on the stillness within the shack. He listened for the slightest sound, watched for any hint of movement that might signal the anticipated ambush.

A stirring in the nearby undergrowth jolted Hood back to the present. Adrenaline surged, his heartbeat quickened, and he instinctively reached for the shotgun. Foliage parted and a watchful doe stepped into the weedy yard. She warily surveyed her surroundings as a fawn, then another, joined her in the clearing.

Hood relaxed and waited for them to cross the property and disappear again into the woods before restarting his cruiser.

As he drove back to the courthouse, he thought about Westerman, who had said being sheriff was like trying to maintain a balance between satisfaction and disappointment. Sometimes you get to help people, Westerman would say, and sometimes people get hurt.

The gunshot wounds inflicted by Heath Schrock didn't kill Westerman—at least, not immediately. The sheriff was admitted and treated at Huhman County Hospital, where he healed physically and eventually was discharged. But Hood sensed his boss never really recovered. Westerman's passion for the job gradually diminished, and he died from a "coronary event" months after the shooting and months before Heath Schrock faced punishment for his crime.

The ambush Hood had anticipated nine years ago within the gloomy shack had never come.

During their search, Hood and Wally found Heath lying in a fetal position and bleeding on a tattered mattress in the corner of a back bedroom. He had been severely beaten — not by sheriff's deputies, but by his own father.

Schrock was among the first juveniles in the state to be certified to stand trial as an adult. He pleaded guilty to a charge of assault with a deadly weapon and was sentenced to prison.

Now he was free.

Hood sat at his desk, staring blankly at the newspaper he had opened, but was not reading. His thoughts remained with the Schrocks and the showdown at their shack. The prevailing public sentiment at the time was that Hood and Wally had nearly killed the teen in retaliation for shooting Sheriff Westerman. Initially, Hood had been upset about being blamed for something he hadn't done, but he realized public perception wasn't always rooted in reality.

The reality he couldn't shake was he had killed Bobby Schrock. During Hood's more than 20 years as a law enforcement officer — as a deputy and as sheriff — he had fired a gun only once in the line of duty. Hood still picked at the scab of the fatal shooting. He questioned what he could have done differently. Should he have waited for additional backup? Would a greater show of force have resulted in a different outcome?

His self-inquisition was interrupted by Wally, who asked, "You busy?" Hood looked up to where his chief deputy stood in the open doorway. "C'mon in." He refolded the newspaper and set it on the desktop.

"Maggie said you were checking out the Clarke Junction Levee. How's it holding up?"

Hood shrugged. "I'm no expert, but it looked pretty solid to me."

"Good. Guess who was checked in to the Wallendorf-Astoria last night?" Wally asked, using his customary euphemism for the county jail.

The question seized Hood's attention. "Don't tell me — Heath Schrock."

"Nope. Ansel Creighorn."

Hood sighed audibly. "Who'd he beat up this time?"

"Nobody. Actually, he got his ass kicked — dislocated shoulder, lost a tooth, got his nose bloodied."

Hood folded his hands atop the paper and focused his attention on Wally. "Tell me about it."

"Wish I knew more. Art and I responded to a 9-1-1 call at The Sportsmen's, but not before the EMTs had come and gone. According to them, Ansel was ambling around like a wounded bear when they got there. They tried to talk to him, but he was pretty drunk and kept threatening to get somebody he called that 'punk'—didn't even know the guy's name. Finally they got Ansel in an ambulance and took him to the ER. Art and I stuck around to ask some questions, but you know how it is with that crowd—either nobody saw anything or you get a dozen different versions of what happened. The only thing they seemed to agree on was that he didn't look like the kind of guy who could take Ansel."

Hood nodded.

Wally related what he knew about the fight, the shotgun blast, and Creighorn's arrest for unlawful discharge of a firearm.

"Anybody identify the other guy?"

"Either nobody knows or they're not telling. Art said my brother was there. Herman asked if I was on duty and Art told him I was on my way. He was gone by the time I got there, though. Must have gotten tired of sticking around."

"Art may need to talk to him," Hood said. "In the meantime, let's get some prints on the shotgun, see if we can ID this stranger."

"Already at the crime lab."

"Good. Who was working at The Sportsmen's last night?"

"Lester said Shep was in the basement when the fight started. Some new gal who was waiting tables wasn't much help, and Lisa was tending bar, but all we got from her was attitude. Course, you know how she feels about us."

"I do," Hood said. About two years ago, Hood and Wally had arrested her husband Buddy for a convenience store robbery—a step up in offenses from his history of burglary and stealing. Buddy had pleaded guilty and been sentenced to five years' imprisonment. "I may go talk to her," Hood said.

"Good luck."

"In the meantime, I think I'll visit our guest. Maybe he'll be more forthcoming this morning."

"Good luck with that, too."

Hood studied his deputy. "You look tired. Why don't you go home and get some sleep?"

"I will. I am. I just wanted to give you an update."

"Get some rest," Hood advised as he arose from his desk, "and I'll go give Ansel a wake-up call."

"He'll be grouchy and hung over."

"Ansel's always grouchy or hung over," Hood observed, "except when he's drunk."

Hood held two white disposable cups filled with coffee as the jailer opened the door to Creighorn's cell.

The giant reclined on his bunk. His left arm, immobilized in a sling, lay across his massive chest. Although his eyes were closed and he remained motionless, Hood sensed Creighorn was awake.

"Room service," Hood said, lifting one cup slightly. "Rise and shine, Ansel."

The prisoner sat up on his bunk, a movement that brought a grimace of pain to his battered face. He accepted the cup, stared at the welts on the sheriff's face and asked, "What the hell happened to you?"

"Could ask you the same thing."

"Punk cold-cocked me and your guys tossed me in jail."

"Heard you discharged a firearm inside The Sportsmen's."

"Just tryin' to put a little scare in the punk who jumped me. Gun wouldn't have gone off if he didn't whack the barrel."

"Know the guy?" Hood asked.

"No."

"Ever seen him before?"

"No."

"How'd it start?"

"Got nothing to do with you," Ansel growled. "Ain't nothing I can't take care of."

Hood glared at him. "You've got a bad attitude, Ansel. I don't need you taking it out there," he said, gesturing beyond the cell door.

"And I know my rights. You can hold me twenty hours before you cut me loose or charge me, which means settin' bond. Either way, I'm outta here."

"Arrest report's been filed with the prosecutor. Charges are up to him. In the meantime, enjoy the accommodations." Hood stood, then added, "And the complimentary coffee."

CHAPTER

8

By late morning, the rain had stopped, permitting sunlight to peek among intermittent clouds. Hood entered The Sportsmen's, waited for his eyes to adjust to the dim interior, and examined the blast of ceiling damage.

He had called ahead to determine Lisa's work schedule and found her setting tables for the anticipated lunch crowd. A half dozen bar stools already were occupied by retirees and unemployed barflies who habitually started their day — and likely would spend the remainder of it — at the bar.

"Hi, Lisa," Hood greeted when she noticed him approach.

"Sheriff." Her tone was cool, terse.

"I'm trying to find out more about what happened last night — with Creighorn, I mean."

"Already told your deputy what I know." She moved to another table, where she arranged silverware and napkins quickly and proficiently.

Hood followed. "Can we sit and talk for a minute?"

"I'm on the clock, and there's nothing to tell. If talking makes you feel like you're doing your job, go ahead."

Hood frowned. "Do you know the guy Creighorn got into it with?"

"Never seen him before last night."

"He's never been in here before?"

"Not while I've been on duty."

"What did he look like?"

"Average."

"Anything distinguishing—height, weight, facial hair, tattoos?"

"Nope."

"What color was his hair?"

"Brown." She paused, then added, "I think."

"Eyes?"

"Two."

Hood sighed. "Very funny."

"I wasn't gazing into his eyes, Sheriff. I served him a beer. Creighorn tried to whack him with a cue stick, and all hell broke out. End of story."

Hood scratched the back of his neck. "I'm just trying to understand. I figure you're scraping to make ends meet, working all hours of the day and night. That's tough under any circumstances. But you've got a guy like Creighorn as one of your regulars, and lots of folks know better than to even come through that door. Must make tips hard to come by."

"I do all right—considering I'm a single mom with a husband in prison."

Hood hesitated. "Buddy did the crime. I don't apologize for doing my job. But right now we can help each other. I've got Creighorn in jail on a weapons violation. He's got a bad case of vengeance, and I don't want to turn him loose. If I ask the prosecutor to charge him, he'll want to know what kind of case he can make. That means witnesses. If I can't produce, neither will he."

"So get some witnesses."

"I'm told Shep was downstairs. Didn't see any of it."

"Then get somebody else. Place was packed last night."

"C'mon, Lisa," Hood said, trying to reason rather than beg. "You know what this crowd's like. But you, you've got something to gain. With Creighorn's record, I figure we can put him away for a while. But if you won't testify, he'll walk and he'll be back here tonight, and tomorrow night and every night after that until somebody really gets—"

Lisa slammed a fistful of silverware onto a tabletop, where it clanged and clattered, drawing the attention of several squint-eyed barflies. "You're really a piece of work, Sheriff, you know that? What do you take me for? You're helping me? What a joke. First, I told you I don't know anything, but even if I did, you think I'd stiff Creighorn? He'll make bond. You think I want him pissed at me?"

"We'll argue for a high bond."

"He owns an excavating company, for crissakes. You can't set bond high enough on a weapon's charge."

Hood knew she was right. "Okay," he said, "but if you find out who this mystery man is, or if he comes around again, I'd appreciate a call."

She picked up the silverware and moved to another table.

Hood left with no expectation she would call.

* * * * *

"Hello. My name is Allison and I'll be your server this evening." She lit the wick of the small oil lamp centered on the table. "May I start you with something to drink?"

"Want to share a bottle of wine?" David Grimm asked his wife, who sat across from him in the booth at Derek's, an upscale restaurant in western Huhman County.

"I think I'll just have a glass of the Pinot," Cheryl answered. The glazed look in her husband's eyes revealed he already was on the cusp of intoxication. Since he had lost his job, he had advanced the start of his daily drinking from the cocktail hour to early afternoon.

"And I'll have a Grey Goose on the rocks," David told the waitress. He folded the wine list and handed it to her.

"Very good," Allison said. She retreated to the bar.

The couple shared an uncomfortable silence. Cheryl focused on the movements of colorful fish darting and drifting in the clear water of the large aquarium positioned on a stand across the aisle from their booth. A personal trainer would be impressed by Cheryl's well-toned physique. At age 45 and the mother of two sons, she retained the features of her younger self—shapely legs, taut abdomen, and firm breasts and buttocks. Her husband, David, did not share her passion for diet, exercise, or drinking in moderation. He was a large man who had let his once-athletic body become fleshy and flabby. In the six weeks since he lost his lucrative job as an investment counselor, he had descended into indolence and self-indulgence.

"So," David asked, "how's work?"

"Fine." Cheryl shrugged.

Further conversation was forestalled by Allison's return. The server placed their drinks before them, recited the specials, and took their orders before vanishing into the kitchen.

Silence resumed until David said, "Real estate market's soft right now. Any prospects?"

As if on cue to interrupt, Allison returned, delivered a basket of bread sticks, and positioned a plate before each diner.

"Josh and I took a commercial developer to lunch today." Cheryl picked up a bread stick and nibbled. "He's interested in putting a strip mall in—"

"You and Josh?"

Cheryl laid the partially eaten bread stick on her plate. She held up her hands, palms open. "Look, I know how you feel—"

"You and Josh," he repeated, his voice louder. "What did I tell you about you and Josh having lunch together?"

"It was a business lunch. With a client."

"Did you have the *Pinot*?" David said, his tone both sarcastic and hostile. "Look, I know guys like Josh. They're only interested in one thing."

"Stop it," Cheryl said, a plea, not a demand. "That's absurd. He's my boss, he's ten years older than me, and we were entertaining a client." She shook her head. "I am not having this conversation."

"You *are* having this conversation. You're not in the entertainment business. You're in the real estate business. I won't have my wife—" He stopped in mid-sentence as Cheryl slid toward the edge of the bench seat. David reached across the table and seized her wrist in a vice-like grip. As she stood and pulled away, he used her momentum to help him to his feet.

"Let go of me."

He tightened his grip, signaling defiance.

Cheryl laughed involuntarily. "You are so drunk."

David staggered, twisting and pulling her wrist as he lost his balance. Her anguished shriek prompted him to release her, and he flailed helplessly—in seeming slow motion—waving his arms wildly as he toppled backward. A clamor of breaking glass and gushing water followed as David, the aquarium, and its stand crashed to the floor.

Water spread and soaked the carpet. Scattered tropical fish flopped on the floor, their gills pulsing. Cheryl winced in pain, bent forward, and cradled her injured wrist against her abdomen. David lay on his back, scanning the horrified faces of other restaurant patrons who had swiveled their heads to determine the cause of the calamity. Allison and Derek, the owner, rushed to the scene.

What followed was a bizarre blend of comedy and agony. Cheryl retreated to the booth, sat, and suffered silently, while Allison fetched a pitcher of water and attempted to rescue the fish. Derek demanded an explanation from David, who seemed stupefied. After intermingled discussions, excuses, and apologies, David shambled to his feet and insisted on paying for the damages. Derek accepted the offer, but instructed Allison to summon an ambulance. He also decided to call the sheriff's department, in the event a report was needed for an insurance claim. By the time the chief deputy arrived at the scene, he learned from the owner that a remorseful David Grimm had accompanied his wife to the Huhman County Hospital emergency room. At Derek's request, Wally took statements from the owner and from Allison, and filed a report.

Amid the incessant drone of the motor and bursts of staccato screaming, the metal tentacles of the Octopus whirled and thrashed, spinning, twirling, and bouncing excited children up, down, and around.

Hood and Elizabeth stood in their small booth, wedged between the carnival ride and a silver trailer that had been converted into a cotton candy stand. They had erected a canopy to shield them from a persistent drizzle as they stood behind a folding table with a sign that read: SADD: Students Against Destructive Decisions. Hood wasn't certain when the Huhman County chapter of the national organization had been founded, but, as sheriff, he supported the group's message. As a father, he also had encouraged his daughter to join when she was still in middle school. Later, when his drinking became excessive, he recognized his endorsement of the group's message was the height of hypocrisy.

Hood scanned the muddy midway and lamented what the county fair had become. Like most Midwestern county fairs, it had originated as an exhibition and competition for livestock and produce. Hood recalled attending the fair as a boy, when his father would bring the prize of his pumpkin patch and often earn a ribbon, and his mother was considered the person to beat in the rhubarb pie category.

Young Francis, a member of 4-H, spent his afternoons among the livestock and always elected to show Curly, who had become a family pet. Francis and his father had nursed the ailing piglet back to health, and although neither Hood nor his father broached the topic, both understood that Curly was not destined for market. Curly was hardly a show-stopper—although he once won honorable mention—but was popular and always drew a chorus of cheers from relatives and friends.

The livestock and produce exhibitions now were relegated to a pair of run-down pole barns at the far corner of the fairgrounds. The newer pavilions were reserved for beer gardens, arm-wrestling competitions, and chainsaw sculpting. And the show arena was the venue for aging rock bands, country-western performers, monster trucks, and tractor pulls featuring high-horsepower machines completely alien to any farmer's field.

Hood's parents also were gone. His father, who had died seven years before from rapid and painful pancreatic cancer, had lived to see his son become sheriff and to express both his pride and his love. A series of strokes killed Hood's mother less than two years previously. Her funeral marked the last time Hood had seen his lone sibling. His older sister was an educator who lived in New Jersey and had a family of her own.

Hood inhaled an odor of cotton candy and winced. He missed the aroma of freshly baked pies, clusters of garden-grown herbs and spices, even the pungent scent of manure. He also missed his parents and his sister. His in-laws were kind and caring, and they had all but adopted him, but it wasn't the same. He watched some children scamper along the midway, undaunted by the drizzle, although few adults ventured beyond the shelter of the beer gardens. He glanced at his daughter, who was fidgeting with two refrigerator magnets bearing the organization's acronym and slogan.

Hood brushed his fingers through his close-cropped hair. "Slow night," he said.

"Uh huh." Elizabeth stuck the two magnets together, then peeled them apart.

"Want some cotton candy?"

"I'm okay."

Hood smiled. Elizabeth's choices had pleased, and surprised, him. He had expected her—at some point—to dismiss the SADD group as lame. She hadn't. He also had anticipated she would find an excuse to avoid joining him in the booth. She was a rising sophomore, and he knew she faced possible ridicule for promoting a drug and alcohol-free message at a fair popular among her peers. And yet, here she was.

"Is that Deputy Wallendorf?" she asked.

Hood followed her gaze and watched his chief deputy approach. Wally had pulled up his shirt collar to repel the drizzle. The trio exchanged greetings, and Wally accepted an invitation to step inside the shelter of the canopy. He squeezed into the already cramped confines.

"Any news on our mystery man?" Hood asked his deputy.

"Which one—the one from the river or The Sportsmen's?"

"Either."

"Nothing yet," Wally said. "You get anything from Lisa?"

"Just attitude," Hood said. He felt Elizabeth tug on his sleeve.

"Daddy, do you know that man?" she asked as she pointed toward the corner of one of the newer pavilions.

Hood caught a momentary glimpse of someone in a hooded rain poncho watching from the corner of the building before groups of passers-by blocked his line of sight. When the people cleared, the watcher was gone.

"Stay here," Hood instructed. He exited the booth, hurried across the muddy midway and disappeared around the corner of the building where the watcher had been.

Moments later, he returned to the booth.

"What?" Wally asked.

"Nothing," Hood said. He frowned. "He was gone."

"Someone you know?" Wally pressed.

"Can't be sure," Hood said.

"Is everything okay, Daddy?" Elizabeth asked.

"Everything's fine," Hood said. He hoped he sounded convincing.

CHAPTER
9

Hood greeted Maggie, poured coffee for himself, refilled her cup and asked, "Did Corrections send an updated picture of Heath Schrock?"

"There may be an attachment to the email I printed about his release. Hold on."

Hood watched her deftly navigate the computer programs. He knew he had failed to embrace technology and, at times like this, he couldn't help but feel inferior to Maggie, who eagerly adapted to change despite being significantly older. "Nope," she said. "No attachments."

"See if they can send me a recent photo of him."

"Or," Maggie said, "if they've got a digital image, I'll have them email it and I can print it."

"Fine," Hood said. "And just so you know, I cut Creighorn loose yesterday. No charges."

"I noticed he wasn't on the jail roster this morning."

Hood shrugged. "Prosecutor said he wasn't interested, said Creighorn could claim he didn't intend to discharge the gun, he was only bringing it in to show someone and it went off when the other guy whacked it."

"I don't believe that any more than you do."

"Doesn't matter what I believe. Matters what we can prove, and the PA thinks it'd be damn little in this case."

Hood walked to his office, stood behind his desk, and scanned the front page of the newspaper. The lead story again focused on the flood, but offered little new information. He read more about "valiant efforts" by flood victims and community volunteers, then shifted his attention to the reports — a non-injury accident, trespassing, domestic assault with injury. Hood focused on the names, David and Cheryl Grimm, then read Wally's narrative before carrying the report next door to his chief deputy's office.

"You took this report on the disturbance at Derek's?" Hood asked.

Wally looked up from his computer. "Yeah. It was over when I got there. Talked to Derek and a waitress. Some couple got into an argument, and she ended up with a sprained wrist and he tripped and knocked over a large aquarium. Derek said he knows them, and the guy offered to cover the damages, so he's good with that."

"I went to the ER," Wally added, "and talked to —" he hesitated, searched his memory, "what's her name?"

"Cheryl Grimm."

"Yeah, Cheryl. She said it was just a husband-and-wife thing that escalated. She didn't want to make a complaint, said it was no big deal."

Hood's silence prompted Wally to ask, "You know her?"

Hood nodded. "I dated her in high school. She was Cheryl Verslues then."

"I didn't know you dated her," Wally said. "She was a fox—she's still good looking, by the way—but I always thought she went steady with that jock, that David, what's his name?"

"Grimm."

"Oh," Wally said, making the connection. "The husband."

Hood nodded.

"Francis," Maggie interrupted, as she appeared in the doorway. "Loeffelman just sent this over. I thought you'd want to see it right away." She handed him several sheets of paper.

Hood scanned the documents. "Finally."

"What is it?" Wally asked.

"It's the ID on the body you two pulled from the river," Maggie answered.

"Who is he?"

"Name's Travis Haulenbach." Hood studied the dual mug shots—full face and profile. Haulenbach was not a handsome man. His narrow eyes were set close together, his nose was wide and flat, and his crooked teeth protruded from behind thin lips. Hood read the narrative of Haulenbach's physical description, which matched both his own observations and the data from Loeffelman's report. He flipped to a second page and perused the background information. Haulenbach was a Maryland native with a history that sketched the portrait of a drifter—no permanent address, no occupation—and petty criminal. He had been jailed in Pennsylvania, Ohio, and southeastern Missouri for burglary and stealing offenses. He also had served eighteen months of a three-year prison term in Illinois for stealing a car. His only known relatives were his former legal guardians—an uncle and aunt, Ethan and Gertrude Harris—in Annapolis, Maryland.

Hood passed the documents to Wally and said, "Meet Travis Haulenbach." He turned to Maggie and continued, "We'll have to make contact with Annapolis authorities so they can break the news to the relatives. Then we'll need to make arrangements—"

"Wait," Wally interrupted. "I think I know this guy."

Hood and Maggie turned to face him.

"How?" Hood asked.

"I think this is the guy who was working with my brother this spring." Wally looked from the photograph to his boss and added, "Out at the cemetery."

Heath Schrock entered the apartment with two six-packs of beer, one pinned under an arm and the other in his hand. Ronnie sat, eyes closed, on the threadbare sofa; Freddie sat in the chair, smoking a joint.

"Fucking stinks in here," Heath said as he set the six-packs on the coffee table, pushing a greasy pizza box and drug paraphernalia onto the floor. He removed a beer can from the package and popped the top, prompting Ronnie to open his eyes.

"Here, cousin," Heath said, handing the beer to Ronnie. He removed a second beer from the plastic rings.

"If you don't like it, you don't have to stay here, man," Freddie said.

Heath hurled the beer can, hard, at Freddie's head. He ducked, and the can exploded against the plaster wall behind him. Foamy beer cascaded down the wall. Freddie jumped from the chair. "What the fuck, man?"

Heath glared at him, said nothing.

"You don't even live here, man," Freddie continued. "The only reason I'm letting you stay here is because of your cousin."

Heath removed another beer. He popped the top and Freddie flinched. "You're letting me stay here?" he asked, repeating Freddie's words as a menacing question.

"Yeah, man," Freddie said, a hint of fear replacing the anger in his tone.

"You say you are letting me stay here?" Heath said again, a staccato pause punctuating each word.

"Hey, Heath," Ronnie interjected. "Let's all just chill, okay? Freddie didn't mean nothin'."

"What did you mean, Freddie?" Heath asked. "You mean I'm not welcome here?"

"Freddie didn't mean that," Ronnie answered. "Freddie's just high. He didn't mean nothin'."

"Let him answer," Heath said to his cousin, although his gaze remained on Freddie.

"It's just, you know, man, this is my place," Freddie said.

"And I'm your guest," Heath said. "Right."

"Yeah," Freddie agreed.

"Then you should be more courteous to your guest. Right?"

Freddie shrugged. "Yeah, I suppose."

"Then smoke that shit outside from now on," Heath said, "or I'll nail you to a fuckin' tree in the backyard."

Hood was running late. He had invited Linda and Elizabeth to the house for family pizza night, but the take-out line at The Pizza Joint was longer, and slower, than he anticipated. When he finally turned into his driveway, the sight of his wife's van and a department cruiser parked nose to tail at the curb confused him. He relaxed, however, when he heard the melody of the piano duet emanating from the window. Elizabeth was a competent pianist, but Hood knew the arrangement exceeded her ability.

He had suggested the family gathering because Elizabeth had been on his mind. The incident at the county fair had been unnerving, but not as troubling as working the scene of a one-vehicle accident on state highway 179 the previous day. If Mother Nature created an amusement ride—worthy of five tickets, at least—it would be the narrow, snaky, treacherous segment of 179 just south of the Huhman County line.

Hood wasn't the first to respond and the wreck wasn't within his jurisdiction, but he lingered at the scene while firefighters used a "jaws of life" hydraulic tool to cut a teenage girl from the passenger seat of the twisted metal that retained little resemblance to the Ford Focus it had been. Even if the girl survived, Hood guessed she would face new challenges.

He balanced two medium pizzas in his left hand, twisted the knob of the unlocked front door, and entered. He looked into the family room at the backs of the mismatched duo seated on a broad bench facing an upright piano. Elizabeth's slender form was dwarfed by her playing partner Deputy Lester Stackhouse, who topped six feet in height and weighed about 230 pounds. Their flesh tones roughly reflected the colors on the piano keyboard; Lester's skin was nearly as black as the sharps and flats, while Elizabeth's complexion resembled the ivory keys.

Elizabeth mechanically repeated the bass line of the twelve-bar blues progression, while Lester's massive hands danced deftly along the keyboard, producing spontaneous, but complementary, phrasings.

Hood knew Lester felt he owed his boss a debt of gratitude, despite Hood's efforts to clear the slate. Lester had been a standout defensive guard in high school and college, and was touted as an early-round draft pick for the National Football League. A series of knee injuries, however, sidelined any promise of a pro career. Although Lester was greeted with much adulation upon his return to Huhman County, the attention was short-lived and career opportunities negligible. When Lester appeared in Hood's office in need of a job, the sheriff handed him an application for a vacant deputy's position, followed by an interview and a job offer. Not until later did Hood learn the depth of his deed; Lester attributed his renewed sense of self-worth to the sheriff's willingness to give him a chance. Although they had worked together for nearly seven years, Hood recalled few occasions when Lester had visited his home.

"Hi, Daddy," Elizabeth said, turning and greeting him as the notes faded.

"That sounded great," Hood said.

"Did you know Deputy Stackhouse's grandfather was a famous musician?" she asked, gesturing toward Lester as he stood.

"I didn't know that."

"Well," Lester said, with customary humility, "I don't know if famous is the word, but he made a decent living doing session work for some Memphis recording studios back in the day. Even got his name on some albums."

"Can you join us for pizza?" Hood asked his deputy.

"Oh, no. I gotta run."

Hood was puzzled. "Is there something you needed to see me about?"

"No, no," Lester replied. "My piano's being worked on and I was in the area, so I thought I'd stop by. Hope you don't mind me playing a few tunes with Elizabeth."

"Not at all. Anything that gets her to practice more."

"Daddy," Elizabeth protested.

"Well," Lester said. "Guess I'll shove off."

"Sure you can't stay?" Hood asked. "There's plenty."

"I'm sure."

They exchanged good-byes, and Elizabeth walked Lester to the door and thanked him, while Hood joined Linda in the kitchen.

"That was a surprise," he said as he set the boxes in the center of the table.

"You're telling me," she said.

"You weren't expecting him?"

"No. I just assumed you invited him."

Some puzzle pieces, Hood thought, obviously were missing.

CHAPTER 10

The hilltop site of Our Lady of Help Catholic Church, under normal circumstances, commanded a panoramic view of the Missouri River and fertile bottomland that stretched to the bluffs beyond. Now it stood as a sentry to devastation. Hood parked in the church lot, and he and Wally silently assessed the transformation of the landscape. A wooden barricade blocked the narrow, winding road that led from the church to the low-lying cemetery, now inundated with muddy floodwaters. In addition, the Vossen farm and a portion of the Stuckenschnieders' vast soybean acreage were under water.

They exited and walked toward the church.

"Linda and Elizabeth came over for pizza last night," Hood said.

"Good. I'm glad you guys are able to keep the lines of communication open. You know I'm pulling for a reconciliation."

"Thanks, but guess who I found there playing piano with Elizabeth?" Hood asked.

"No idea. Who?"

"I think you know," Hood challenged.

"Lester?" Wally ventured, his expression sheepish.

"Exactly. So how many deputies did you recruit to watch over my family?"

"They mostly volunteered," Wally said.

"Look, I appreciate what you did, but we've got an entire county to protect. Tell me you'll put to a stop to it."

"I'll pass the word."

"Thanks," Hood said.

"But," Wally said, as they arrived at a side entrance, "I can't control what they do in their spare time."

Hood's expression reflected his reluctant acceptance as he opened and held the door for his chief deputy, then followed him inside.

Wally, who was familiar with the church and acquainted with Mrs. Sandbothe, guided his boss to one in a series of small offices, occupied by a petite, elderly woman whose severe expression seemed designed to show her meticulous pride both in her appearance and in her role in the parish.

After Wally made introductions, Hood extended his hand and said, "Pleased to meet you. We spoke on the phone a few days ago. About the body we retrieved."

"I recall," she said. "Did you find out who he is?"

Hood handed her a photograph of Travis Haulenbach.

Mrs. Sandbothe's expression registered both surprise and recognition. "Goodness," she said, raising her fingers to her lips. "He worked here this spring."

"That's why we're here," Wally said, followed by Hood's question, "What was his job, exactly?"

Mrs. Sandbothe explained he had been hired—on the recommendation of Wally's brother, Herman—to help maintain the church and its grounds, including the cemetery. She said

Haulenbach was paid an hourly rate and was under Herman's supervision. He had been at the job about two months before Herman reported Haulenbach had stopped showing up for work. She and Herman assumed he had moved on to another job or another town.

Hood pressed for more details, and Mrs. Sandbothe produced a personnel file that included Haulenbach's completed job application, the standard paperwork for employment, and time slips reflecting dates from early March to April. Hood jotted Haulenbach's home address in a notebook and mentally calculated about four weeks had elapsed since the man's absence was noticed.

The sheriff asked Mrs. Sandbothe her impression of Haulenbach, but she balked. "I hardly knew the man. You'd better talk to Herman."

"Is he working today?" Wally asked.

"He should be out back. We're relocating the cemetery to higher ground — on a tract we own behind the church. We've got lots of reburials, and the board decided we certainly don't want something like this to ever happen again."

Hood and Wally exited the church and followed a muddy lane for about the length of three football fields. The lane took them beyond a copse of trees that largely shielded the church from a large open area cleared of trees and shrubs. Herman was leaning against an earth-moving machine, wiping sweat from his forehead and sipping from a plastic water bottle.

"Hey, brother," Wally greeted as they approached.

Herman looked up and startled reflexively. "Oh man, don't sneak up on me like that."

"What d'ya got, a guilty conscience or something?"

"No man. It's just I been busting my ass all morning, and I thought you were the pastor, just when I decide to take a break."

"I said 'brother.'"

"That's what he calls me, too. Brother Herman, as in all men are brothers."

As they bantered, Hood assessed the two siblings. Herman was almost the mirror image of his big brother. Herman shared Wally's lean frame, angular facial features, and thick, unruly hair. Wally was the taller of the two, perhaps by an inch, while Herman was more muscular, with the sinewy tone developed through manual labor.

Hood took the photo of Travis Haulenbach from his pocket and handed it to Herman. "Know this guy?"

Herman hesitated. "Yeah," he said as he continued to examine the picture. "He worked with me here for a while. Name's Travis — Hallenbeck, or something like that."

"Haulenbach," Hood corrected.

"Yeah," Herman said. He handed the photo back to the sheriff. "Is he in trouble or something?"

"When did he work here?"

"March, April." Herman looked at his brother. "We had that early spring and I was trying to get the grounds cleaned up in addition to my indoor chores. Plus, I was still redoing the activities room. I just couldn't keep up, so I asked Mrs. Sandbothe if I could get some help—you know, just temporary."

"You hired Travis?" Hood asked.

"No. She did—Mrs. Sandbothe."

"She said you recommended him."

Herman looked pleadingly at his brother. "What's going on?"

"We just need some information," Wally said, his tone reassuring. "Did you recommend him?"

"Yeah," Herman said. He shifted his focus back to Hood. "But I didn't hire him. I don't have the authority to hire folks."

"So why'd you recommend him?" Hood asked. "Had you known him a while?"

"Not really." Herman shrugged. "I just met him in February when he started coming to The Sportsmen's. I think he knew Ansel from before, though, because sometimes—"

"Ansel Creighorn?" Hood asked.

"Yeah. I guess they knew each other as kids—Ansel grew up somewhere in Maryland, you know—because they'd talk about stuff that happened a long time ago. Anyway, this Travis guy started coming to the bar, which is where we usually hang out after work to have a beer, maybe shoot some pool, throw some darts. One night, after I got to know him a little, me and Travis were shooting pool and he said he was looking for work. I needed some help and he seemed like an okay guy, so I put in a word with Mrs. Sandbothe."

"Why'd he quit?" Hood asked.

"He didn't quit, exactly. He just stopped showing up. From what I gathered, he was kind of a drifter. I figured he just moved on." Herman sipped water. "I got no idea where he is if you guys are looking for him."

"We're not," Hood said. "We found him. He's dead."

Herman shook his head and exhaled a long breath. "Jeez, what happened?"

"We're not sure, exactly."

"How'd he die?"

"It's still under investigation," Hood said. "Ever been to his place?"

"Dropped him off once or twice. It's an old apartment building on the east side. I don't remember the street or number. I don't know if I could find it again. Mrs. Sandbothe's probably got the address."

Hood nodded. "Already got it from her. What else can you tell me about him?"

"Not a lot. Drank too much and was hung over most mornings. Had to stay on top of him to get any work out of him. Afternoons were better." Herman shrugged. "Just a guy, you know. Still, it's weird to think he's dead."

"Different topic," Hood said. "I'm told me you were at The Sportsmen's the night Ansel Creighorn got his shoulder dislocated, but you left before—"

"That was some crazy shit," Herman interrupted.

"So why'd you leave before deputies got a chance to take your statement?"

"I figured you had enough witnesses. The place was a

circus with people talking about the guy who decked Ansel, trying to guess who he was."

"Did you recognize him?"

"Well, I'm not really sure, but I thought it might be Bobby Schrock's kid, but I ain't seen him in a long time and, besides, he's doin' time."

"Not anymore," Hood said. "He's out."

"No shit?" Herman said. "Could've been, then."

"Okay," Hood said to Herman. "That's all for now, but we may need to talk to you again."

"Yeah, sure," Herman said.

Wally playfully slapped his brother on the shoulder. "Now get back to work, you goldbricker."

"Yeah, right." Herman climbed aboard the earthmover and started the engine.

Hood and Wally walked away. When they got back to the parking lot, Hood said, "Well, everything Mrs. Sandbothe and your brother told us pretty well matches." When Wally failed to reply, Hood added, "What do you think?"

Wally's lips tightened into a puzzled look. "Something's not right," he said.

Hood had sensed the same thing.

"What's up," Ronnie Schrock asked his cousin, who was leaning over the front fender into the engine compartment of the old pickup.

Heath adjusted a screw on the carburetor. "Truck runs like shit," he said, without looking up.

"Was all I could do to get it running," Ronnie said, more explanation than apology. "Why don't you get that heap inspected and registered and you can help me with my landscaping business?"

"Landscaping?" Heath repeated. He backed out from under the hood and stretched. "You're no landscaper. You cut grass and brush and haul it off."

"Still, I could use some help," Ronnie said.

"In this heat and humidity?" Heath indulged in a brief laugh in answer to his own question.

"Make some money," Ronnie said. "Freddie's gonna be asking when you're gonna start chipping in for rent."

"Fuck Freddie."

"I got a pretty sweet deal living here," Ronnie said. "You wouldn't wanna screw that up for me, would you?"

"Don't worry." Heath punched his cousin lightly on the biceps. "Besides, you're a Schrock," he continued, his playful smile gradually morphing into an adamant challenge. "You and I are blood. We stick together. Right?"

"Sure. Of course," Ronnie said, realizing he may have hesitated a moment too long to sound convincing.

"Good, because I need a favor."

"Okay."

"Need to borrow your truck for a couple of hours."

Ronnie knew better than to point out his cousin's lack of a driver's license. Instead he said, "Sure. What for?"

"Need to look up somebody."

"Who?"

"What's with all the fucking questions? Can I borrow it or not?"

"Yeah," Ronnie said. "Just curious, is all."

"Well, if you must know, it's a girl I met at a bar the other night."

"Not wasting any time, huh," Ronnie said, grinning.

"It's not like that. She's married to a guy I celled with. He talked about her a lot, where she lives, where she tends bar. I looked her up at The Sportsmen's the other night, and we chatted some."

"'Because if you're looking for what you been missing out on for the last nine—"

"Don't even go there, Ronnie. I can get that anytime, anywhere. This girl's different."

"Sure."

"I'm serious, Ronnie," Heath persisted. "She's got a kid. She's got a job. I wish you could've been there the other night and seen how she handled the shit that went down. She's got class."

"Okay, okay," Ronnie said. He held up his hands in a gesture of surrender. "Keys are by the phone. Help yourself."

Hood descended the stairway leading to the St. Cecilia Catholic Church basement. The lower level served a range of sacred and secular functions, including gymnasium, nursery, wedding reception venue, multi-purpose room, and—on election days—voting precinct. The rectangular grouping of folding tables and chairs indicated the room had been prepared for Recovery Rules, a weekly meeting hosted by Matthew, Hood's sponsor. Although Matthew included 12-step concepts, he didn't stick to them exclusively, and he deviated from the format followed by other groups. Matthew occasionally would invite guest speakers or introduce materials from other disciplines, including organized religion, philosophy, psychology, and medicine. All addicts were welcome. Alcoholics and drug addicts made up the majority of the regulars, but some participants shared their struggles with eating disorders or with gambling or pornography addictions.

Matthew also volunteered for a program called New Opportunities, operated by Huhman County Hospital to offer inpatient detox and intensive outpatient programs for alcoholics and drug addicts. He helped link patients interested in long-term recovery to community resources beyond those provided by the hospital.

As Hood crossed the room, he spotted Matthew in the kitchen making coffee. In the nine months Hood had been attending meetings, he had gotten to know the "regulars." He approached the early arrivals and sat to the left of Mac, one of the venerated "old timers" in the program. The banter and small talk in progress touched on the persistent rains and the respective records of the Cardinals and Royals. The conversation diminished when Matthew approached and set carafes of coffee—one regular and one decaf—on the table. Hood was reminded of a classroom of unruly students becoming silent and attentive when their teacher entered.

"May we open this meeting with a moment of silence for the still-suffering alcoholic," Matthew said, "followed by the Serenity Prayer for those who wish to join in."

Following the cues from others at the tables, Hood bowed his head, but sneaked a peek at the other attendees. They seemed a random representation, as if someone had gone into a shopping mall and rounded up the first dozen or so people—old and young, men and women, well-groomed and scruffy, neatly dressed and disheveled.

"God," Matthew began, followed by other voices joining in ragged unison, "grant me the serenity to accept the things I cannot change, the courage to change the things I can, and the wisdom to know the difference."

Matthew scanned the faces of the dozen or so people seated around the tables. "Before I introduce the topic for tonight, I want to ask if anyone has anything to report— something that happened in the past week, something on your mind or heart, some new challenge?" When no one spoke, Matthew continued, "Okay, I thought tonight we'd talk about how we addicts must come to terms with our past behaviors. It's an ongoing challenge for me, but I've learned some of us carry a much heavier burden, so I asked Chris if he would share a part of his story, and he said he would. Chris."

"Hello. I'm Chris and I'm an alcoholic."

A chorus of greetings followed.

"I don't talk about this a lot, because it sounds like a

'pity me' story, and I don't mean it that way. When I was younger, before I got into recovery, I lived at home with my mom. One night, she had a stroke, but I was so strung out on drugs and alcohol, I couldn't even call for help."

Hood felt the weight of the collective silence in the room.

"The good news is she survived; the bad news is she's partially paralyzed and her speech is slurred. I started my path to recovery the day after it happened. I promised myself I would stay clean and sober, and I would take care of her for as long as she needed me. And I have. That's pretty much it."

"And how long ago did that happen, Chris?" Matthew asked.

"It'll be four years next month."

"Thanks for sharing," Matthew said, triggering similar sentiments from others around the tables.

Next to share was Angie, a single mother who had raised two children during her decades-long battle with alcoholism.

"Angie, alcoholic," she began. "Notice I didn't say 'grateful' alcoholic, like I've heard others refer to themselves. I'm happy for people who feel that way, but I'm not there yet. Don't get me wrong. I'm grateful for where I am now in my recovery, but I'm not grateful for the shit I put other people through, especially my kids." She reached for the carafe, topped her coffee and looked at Chris. "I get it, Chris. I can't undo what I did. I can't just forget it. I've got to find a way to live with it. That's all I've got."

Next up was Mac. He introduced himself, waited for the greetings to diminish, and said, "My past was dominated by selfishness, which—in retrospect—was actually self-deception. I used to blame everyone else for my problems. If my wife didn't do this, if my kids didn't do that. If my boss wasn't so—fill in the blank. There was my way and the wrong way. In recovery, I realized I was blaming other people so I didn't have to change.

"Another thing I've learned is my good intentions weren't reflected in my alcoholic behaviors. I might agree to help you with something, but then I'd get drunk and not show up. I was irresponsible and unreliable. I hurt people and lost self-respect. I ended up lonely and miserable.

"Today, I live in the present. I must acknowledge my past, but I can't live there. It's too dangerous. There's too much guilt, shame, and remorse. If I dwell on it, I'm in danger of seeking relief, and I know my default is alcohol.

"I can't undo what I did as an addict," Mac concluded, "but I can be better today."

The sharing moved to Hood. "Hi, I'm Francis and I'm an alcoholic. I'm just going to listen tonight."

At the conclusion of the meeting, several members remained to wipe tables, fold chairs, and stack them on carts. Eventually, only Hood and Matthew remained in the kitchen, dumping coffee grounds and wiping counters.

"That topic tonight really hit home," Hood said, as he sipped coffee from a disposable cup.

"That happens sometimes."

"I've been dealing with some things from my past lately."

"Uncomfortable things?"

Hood nodded. "I feel like it's crowding me."

"Let's talk about it."

"Okay," Hood said. They sat on stools perpendicular to each other at a stainless-steel food preparation table centered in the kitchen. "Well, now that I think of it, this is probably going to sound silly."

Matthew remained silent, attentive.

"First, there's this woman I haven't been in touch with for years, but her name has come up in a couple recent domestic reports—mostly arguments with her husband. Thing is, she was my childhood sweetheart and the first girl I dated in high school." He sipped coffee. "So, I don't know—"

The ensuing silence prompted Matthew to ask, "You don't know what, exactly?"

"Whether to get involved, I guess. Not involved. That's not the right word. It's just—things didn't end well."

"How did they end?'"

"Another guy came into the picture. He beat me up, humiliated me in front of a bunch of classmates. She dumped me to go out with him. She ended up marrying him, in fact."

Hood looked up from his cup and watched Matthew's lips twist into a crooked frown. "Any thoughts?"

Matthew rested his elbows on the steel surface and tented his hands in front of his mouth. "For me, I'd have to do some self-analysis and examine my motives. I'd ask myself: What am I trying to accomplish here?"

"You know," Hood said, "when I read the report about their fight in their front yard, my initial reaction was to gloat. In high school, they were the prom king and queen, our yearbook called them the couple most likely to succeed."

"Did you feel vindicated, somehow?"

"I think I did, at least at first." Hood looked down at his shoes. "But then I looked at my own life—alcoholic, separated from his family—and I had to take a few steps back."

"Don't beat yourself up, Francis. We're human, with all the feelings and emotions that go with it. Recovery helps us recognize and work on our flaws, but it doesn't always eliminate them."

"I'm beginning to hate this self-analysis."

"It doesn't matter if you hate it. It matters that you continue to do it."

A brief silence ensued until Matthew said, "You said some things from the past. What else?"

"I've talked to you before about Bobby Schrock, the guy I killed years ago when I was deputy. Well, his son just got out of prison and that started me thinking about it all over again. What I could have done different, whether I could have—I don't know."

"You said you and another deputy pulled up to his house in two separate cars and he shot out both windshields. I don't see how you had any other choice."

"I could have waited for more backup. Maybe with a bigger show of force, I could've talked him down."

"Our program also suggests we stay in the present. Living in the past is just second-guessing yourself. You did what you were trained to do. You came under fire and you reacted. For your own peace of mind, it's time to close that case."

Easier said than done, Hood thought.

CHAPTER
11

Hood parked in the lot at Millie's Diner and waited for the downpour to abate.

He shouldered open the door of his cruiser and sprinted through raindrops and puddles. Inside, he shook residual rain from his jacket onto the welcome mat. Wally and Lester were seated in their customary booth hunkered over cups of coffee. As Hood approached and slid onto the bench, Millie appeared, turned a white stoneware cup upright, and filled it from a coffee pot.

"Good morning, Sleeping Beauty," she greeted.

"What?" Hood said, feigning protest. "It's not even seven yet. How long have we been doing this?"

"Just saying," Millie answered. "Wally was here early enough to open the place if he had a key."

"And I'm just saying I'm not late." Hood turned to his deputies. "Right?"

Wally and Lester nodded, with mock obedience.

"If you say so," Millie said. "You boys ready, or you need a few minutes?"

"I'm ready," Wally said, prompting agreement. Each ordered from memory.

After Millie gathered the unnecessary menus and left,

Hood said, "I'm waiting on a call from Maggie. She's trying to track down Haulenbach's landlord." Hood and Wally had visited the apartment after their conversation with Herman the previous day, but no one answered the knock, so Hood had delegated the task of locating the landlord to his dispatcher. Hood sipped coffee and continued, "Any word from the lab on the fingerprints from Creighorn's shotgun?"

"The only definitive prints belong to Creighorn," Wally answered.

"I was afraid of that," Hood said. "I'm going to show Heath's picture, and Haulenbach's, around The Sportsmen's later, see if anybody will confirm Heath was the guy Creighorn called out. Also, I talked to Maryland authorities about notifying next of kin. I got in touch with the Anne Arundel County Sheriff's Department, but they referred me to Annapolis PD. The sheriff's office out there is nothing like here. They're mostly just process servers. They really don't have much law enforcement responsibility. They don't deal with—"

The ringtone of his cell phone interrupted him in mid-sentence. Hood glanced at the readout, told his deputies the caller was Maggie, then answered.

"Found your landlord," she said. "Name's Cristos Papanficus. Owns three buildings on East State Street and lives in apartment A at 312, just a few doors down from Haulenbach's address."

"Thanks," Hood said. "Remind me to promote you to detective."

"It wasn't that hard, Francis, not when you share the same courthouse with the recorder, collector, and assessor, who have property records and plat books."

"Okay, but at least let me bring you a doughnut."

"Thanks anyway, but I'm watching my weight. Oh, and by the way, that address is inside the city limits, so you want to reach out to St. Gotthard PD."

"Not necessary."

"I know it's not necessary," she said, "but it's a courtesy, Francis."

"I'm only talking to a landlord."

"About a murder investigation," Maggie said. "I know you have jurisdiction throughout the county, but I'd consider it a favor if you reached out. Just so there's no hard feelings."

"Okay," Hood conceded.

"Good. Want me to make the call?"

"No, Sauers may be on duty," Hood added, referring to Lt. Gene Sauers, a shift commander for the St. Gotthard Police Department. "Better if I make the call."

He disconnected, updated his deputies on the conversation, and asked, "Where was I?"

"You contacted Maryland authorities," Lester said.

"Right," he said. "I talked to a Captain Winter and told him I'd send the medical examiner's report, identification, and death certificate. The captain's supposed to get back with me after they've notified the aunt and uncle." He paused. "Which reminds me, Loeffelman completed his autopsy, so we can start making arrangements to ship the body."

When he finished, Millie appeared—as if on cue—holding a plate in each hand and deftly balancing a third on her forearm. She put each in its proper place. "I'll bring more coffee," she said. "Anything else?"

"Actually," Hood said, "I'm going to need a doughnut to go."

A light drizzle spattered the windshield as Heath Schrock drove slowly around the lot at Maple Grove Apartments. During his incarceration, Schrock had honed his abilities to be patient and purposeful. After Buddy had shared his memories and a photo of his wife and son, Schrock engaged his cellmate in additional conversations to glean more details about Buddy's family, including the name of their apartment complex. Although Schrock didn't know the specific building or apartment number, he figured Lisa's battered Ford compact car—which he had seen her drive from The Sportsmen's lot—would not be difficult to spot.

He was not quite halfway through the complex when he saw it. He parked his cousin's truck under the shelter of a silver maple tree in a corner of the lot, slumped in his seat, and waited. Schrock likened waiting to doing nothing, and doing nothing reminded him of doing time—biding time, marking time, killing time. He had developed a habit of rhyming nonsense syllables as something to do while waiting. Schrock wondered at times if the rhyming developed from the children's books his mother had read to him as a youth.

GHOUL DUTY

"Pukka, lukka, mocka, pocka," Schrock muttered. He rhymed aloud only when he was confident no one was around because, during the times when he was overheard, the typical reaction was what he called "a funny look."

Before his mother died—an accidental drowning in the river, he had been told—she had read aloud to him at bedtimes. He remembered the captivating, sing-song lilt of her voice and sometimes pictured her, tall and graceful, wading in the water with her long, white skirt billowing about her on the surface. He suspected, however, his mother's death may not have been an accident; even a child knows when a parent is wearing a fragile mask of happiness.

The appearance of Lisa yanked him from his musings. She emerged from an apartment building followed by a young boy, and together they ran through raindrops toward her car. Schrock started the truck and followed Lisa's car westbound along Route DD for about two miles before she turned into a Shop 'N' Save. He followed and waited until the mother and son were inside before parking, crossing the lot, and letting the automatic doors welcome him inside the sprawling grocery store. He scanned the checkout lanes quickly before wandering the length of the interior and surveying each aisle.

He located Lisa in the produce section as she dropped the second of two large, ripe tomatoes into a clear plastic bag. She sensed someone approach and, when she looked up and spotted him, her expression revealed surprise.

"Hello again," he greeted.

Before she could reply, the boy, armed with a bunch of celery, ran to her. "What about these, Mom?" he asked, as he displayed the clump of leafy stalks. The boy noticed his mother's gaze was focused on Schrock.

"You must be Corey," Schrock said to the child.

"Cody," Lisa corrected. "This is my son," she said to Schrock. "And this is Mr. Schrock," she added, completing the introduction. She inspected the celery. "This is fine." She watched her son eye Schrock suspiciously. "Thanks, honey."

Schrock noticed in Lisa's expression, for the first time, a trace of apprehension. He extended his hand to the child and said, "Hi, Cody. Nice to meet you."

Cody edged nearer to his mother, but accepted the handshake. "Hi," he said, shyly.

"Mr. Schrock is a friend of your father's," Lisa said, sensing an explanation was needed.

"You know my dad?" Cody asked. His eyes brightened.

"Uh huh," Schrock answered.

"How?" Cody asked.

Schrock looked at Lisa, his questioning expression intended to seek her guidance about how he should answer.

"It's okay," she said. "Cody knows his father's in prison. We visit all the time."

"You were in prison, too?" Cody asked. His tone held no hint of anxiety; instead, it revealed curiosity and consolation that prisoners — like his father — eventually were set free.

"Yeah," Schrock said. He was uncomfortable being quizzed by a child.

"What for?" Cody asked.

Schrock glanced at Lisa, hoping she would intercede. Instead, he sensed she shared her son's interest in his answers.

"Your dad talked about you all the time," Schrock said. "You and your mom both. He was real proud of his family."

"I know," Cody said.

An awkward silence ensued before Lisa suggested to her son, "Why don't you pick out some lettuce for us, too?"

The boy hesitated momentarily. "Okay."

Silence regathered around Schrock and Lisa as they watched Cody examine the produce.

"Well," Schrock said. "Good seeing you. Guess I'd better shove off."

He pivoted, but hadn't taken a step before Lisa asked, "Wanna come for lunch?"

The suddenness of the invitation surprised them both.

Schrock turned back to face her.

"I make a mean BLT," she said.

"You sure?"

"It'll be good for Cody. You can tell him more about his dad. I know he'd like that."

Schrock sensed she also was eager to hear more about Buddy. "Okay," he agreed. He followed Lisa and her son back to the apartment, where the lunch conversation occasionally was punctuated by strained silence, but the BLT, as advertised, was exceptional. Each bite afforded Schrock a blend of salty bacon, juicy tomato, and crisp lettuce layered between the contrasting chilled mayonnaise and warm toast. He tried to recall eating a similarly satisfying meal prior to his diet of prison fare, but without success.

His childhood and adolescence, it seemed, had been bereft of sensory experience. Whenever he reached for his memory, he encountered a void—not a dark abyss, but a persistent and dismal gray. The lone exceptions were recollections of his mother singing, reading, or turning pages displaying colorful characters against bright backgrounds. The voice or image of his father, however, always would intrude, and Schrock would retreat into the dingy recesses of his mind.

His years in prison were contrastingly vivid. His conversation with Lisa and Cody had taken him back inside the walls, but there were too many dangerous corridors they wanted to explore that Schrock refused to enter. He had described Buddy's cell, adorned with pictures of his family and artwork Cody had created. He discussed Buddy's renewed interest in reading, his job in the prison library, and highlights from some of their spring softball games. Other recollections he kept hidden, including the dual indignities Buddy had suffered after he balked at sexual submission; Buddy repeatedly had been beaten as a prelude to forced sodomy. Schrock initially had endured similar brutality but had found a solution. Prison society, he quickly learned, was no different from anywhere else—some people wielded power; others were pawns. In Schrock's prison society, Jimmy Kronk was among the most powerful predators. Kronk led a gang of inmates who fared well within the walls, amassing power and money by selling contraband and protection. Schrock invested in his own safety, and his problem disappeared. Schrock's tormentor lost an eye; the wound came with a warning that if Schrock were molested again, by anyone, further retribution, literally, would be blind.

"Coffee?" Lisa asked.

"Huh?" Schrock said, still deep in his reverie.

"Would you like some coffee?"

"Love some."

"Mom," Cody said, "can I go outside and play?"

"It's raining."

"It stopped."

"You'll get all muddy."

"Just on the swing. Please."

"Only if you wear your boots and only if you stay on the playground."

Schrock recalled the rusty, run-down swing set and monkey bars just outside the building. Cody sprang from his chair, pulled on his boots, and was sprinting for the door when Lisa reminded him to say good-bye to their guest.

"Oh yeah, bye."

"And you can only play for about half an hour," Lisa called after him. "I've got to get ready for work and drop you at Grandma's. Be ready to go when I come out."

"'Kay. Bring my sneakers, please."

As Cody pulled the door closed behind him, Schrock said, "He's a good kid."

"He is, but he's all boy. Decaf okay?"

"Decaf's fine."

Lisa stood and walked to the counter.

"Must be tough," Schrock continued, "raising him by yourself, I mean."

She dumped a final scoop of coffee into the filter, then shrugged. "You do what you have to do. Been that way all my life."

"Tell me about it?" Schrock said—a question, not an affirmation.

"My life?" She exhaled a brief laugh. "Not much to tell."

"What about you and Buddy—how'd you meet?"

"He didn't tell you?"

Schrock shook his head.

"Not surprised. It's no fairy tale, that's for sure. He was probably too embarrassed."

"About what?"

"I was working as a dancer—an exotic dancer, but I was more naked than exotic—and the gentlemen's club where I worked didn't attract many gentlemen. It was a prefab building on a concrete slab off the interstate. Buddy was helping a friend make some deliveries, and they stopped for some R and R and some of the slop we called food, but mostly because his friend liked the view. Buddy and I got to talking during my break, and that's how we hooked up."

The coffee finished brewing just before Lisa ended her story. She poured a cup, set it on the table in front of Schrock, and said, "Here you go. I better start getting ready for work." She disappeared into a bedroom.

Schrock walked to the door and heard the shower come on. He lingered, recalling what his cousin had said. Schrock's sexual experiences had been confined to an awkward encounter with a girl during his sophomore year and the homosexual horrors inflicted on him early in prison life. Was the shower an invitation? He argued the question in his mind. Thoughts of her naked—dancing on stage and now under a cascade of water—aroused him. He considered entering her bedroom, but balked. Would she welcome him or recoil in fear, as from a brute? He would not victimize her; he would do nothing disrespectful. As much as he desired her, he wanted more for her to soften to him. He returned to the table and sipped coffee until she reappeared.

"Got to run," Lisa said. She switched off the coffee maker and lifted the pot.

Schrock stood. "Let me help," he offered as he removed the wet filter containing the grounds.

They moved simultaneously; Lisa spilled coffee from the pot into the sink at the same moment Schrock opened the cabinet below. They stood face to face briefly before Lisa laughed self-consciously and slipped under his arm.

"I've really got to run," she repeated.

Schrock nodded.

Hood parked at the curb in front of 312 East State Street, called the police department, and asked for the shift commander.

"Lieutenant Sauers," a familiar voice answered.

Hood identified himself and the purpose of his call. Sauers, as expected, was officious and curt. Hood always had sensed a disconnect between them. Sauers served as point man whenever an agency requested formation of a special task force, and Hood had served with him in that capacity on previous occasions. The sheriff didn't know whether to attribute Sauers' coolness to something personal or professional. He was aware that some members of the police department—and State Highway Patrol, for that matter— considered the sheriff's department an inferior form of law enforcement, perhaps because its requirements were less rigorous. Whatever the reason, Sauers routinely was arrogant and aloof in the presence of Hood and his employees.

After the call, Hood pocketed the phone and exited his air-conditioned cruiser. A mantle of humidity immediately draped itself over his body and dampened his skin. He pressed the door buzzer twice before he heard footsteps approaching from within. The man who answered the door was short and stocky, with thinning black hair, the shadow of what could be a prodigious beard, and a natural, unaffected smile.

"Yes?" he said, holding the door half open and scrutinizing the sheriff's uniform.

"I'm your sheriff, Francis Hood. I'm looking for Christos Papa—uh."

"Papanficus. Yes, that's me." The landlord spoke quickly, with an accent Hood could not identify. "People call me Papa Chris, or just Papa."

Hood nodded. "I'm here to inquire about one of your tenants — a Travis Haulenbach."

"Yes, yes. He owes me money. You tell him."

"I'm trying to —"

"Owes May rent. You tell him he owes me money."

"Mr. Papa — uh, Papa Chris. Travis Haulenbach is dead."

"Ohhhh," the landlord said, drawing out the syllable as if the tenant's death had solved the mystery of the missing rent.

Hood learned through further questioning that Papa Chris had last seen his tenant sometime in April. He didn't remember the specific date, only that the May rent was late. The landlord said he had called the phone number Haulenbach had provided and knocked on the apartment door on repeated occasions to collect the past-due amount, but had received no answer. Only then did Papa Chris enter the apartment, which he found empty of any personal possessions. He assumed Haulenbach had left without paying and decided it was time to seek a new tenant for the unoccupied apartment.

"Can I see it?" Hood asked.

"Sure." Papa Chris retrieved the key, escorted Hood to the building and unlocked the door to the vacant apartment. As anticipated, it was small and furnished spartanly with older, mismatched pieces. He examined the room visually but touched nothing.

"Did you clean in here?" Hood asked.

"Sure," the landlord said. "Vacuumed, dusted, cleaned bathroom and kitchen. Haven't found new tenant yet."

"Good," Hood said. "Papa Chris, I don't want anyone in here until I can get a forensics team to go over the place. Can you do that?"

"Forensics?"

"Crime lab guys," Hood clarified.

"Man killed by murder?" Papa Chris asked, his tone betraying a hint of anxiety.

"We don't know. That's why we're looking for evidence."

"Okay."

"It may take a few days."

Papa Chris shrugged.

Hood wiped his forehead with his damp handkerchief. "Okay. Let's lock this place up."

The last of the three men seated in a booth at The Sportsmen's handed the photograph back to Hood. "Used to come around here. Ain't seen 'im in a while, though."

"Name's Travis Haulenbach," Hood told the trio as he pocketed the photo. "You guys know who he hung out with, who he avoided? Any enemies? Ever heard anybody make any threats to—?"

"Excuse me," Lisa interrupted as she angled beside Hood. "What's going on?"

"Just showing some pictures around," Hood said. He took out a second photograph, a picture of Heath Schrock, which he intended to pass around next.

"Unless they're pictures of your kids or dogs, you need to stop. You're bothering the customers."

"And you know better," Hood said. "But since you've got a problem, maybe you can help me. Know this guy?" He displayed Schrock's photo to Lisa and saw a flash of familiarity in her expression.

"Why?"

"Has he been in here recently?"

"Why do you think I'd know the answer?"

"Why do you insist on answering my questions with another question?" Hood glanced at the trio grouped around the table, noticed their collective amusement, and walked Lisa to a vacant corner.

"When I asked you the other day if you knew the guy who tangled with Creighorn, you said you'd never seen him before. I just want to know if this is the guy."

"Who is he?" Lisa asked.

"You're doing it again with the questions." Hood inhaled a long breath. "Name's Heath Schrock. He's an ex-con. Got out a few days ago."

Lisa shrugged. "Could be. Hard to tell."

"That's the best you can do?"

"Yeah."

Hood switched photographs and showed her the picture of Travis Haulenbach. "What about this guy?"

"Yeah, I heard you asking those guys in the booth. He used to come in here. Hung out with Creighorn and his bunch — Neil Bowden, your deputy's brother Herman."

"When was the last time you saw him?"

"A month?" she guessed. "Maybe six weeks."

"Can you be more specific?"

"I don't take attendance."

"Any enemies you know of?"

"Why? Did he tangle with somebody, too?"

"Maybe," Hood said. "He's dead."

She processed the statement. "Somebody kill 'im?"

"It's still under investigation."

Lisa drew air through her teeth. "Well," she said. "That sucks."

CHAPTER

12

Hood was on the river, on Ghoul Duty, but his thoughts were scattered. He sat in the bow, pretending to scan the riverbanks, while Wally sat behind him in the stern, piloting the johnboat slowly upstream. After a lengthy silence, Hood said, "Can I ask you something?"

"Sure."

"Are there things in your life you would do over if you could? You know, things you regret?

"I regret I didn't buy that four-by-four pickup Chester Forck was selling last month."

"You know what I mean—things that made a difference in your life."

Wally hesitated several beats, then answered, "I guess I'm one of those guys who figures everything happens for a reason." He shrugged. "You know, you've got to take the good with the bad. Why?"

"No reason," Hood lied. "I've just been rethinking some things lately."

"Like what?"

"Like killing Bobby Schrock, for one."

"You saved our lives," Wally countered. "Bobby fired at us first."

"Maybe I could've taken him down without—"

"And maybe we wouldn't be talking about this now because one or both of us would be dead."

Hood exhaled a sigh.

"I mean it, Francis," Wally said. "What you did—"

The ringtone on Hood's cell phone halted the conversation. He looked at the display, which read: "Caller unknown." He pressed the green icon and said, "This is your sheriff."

"There's a big propane tank loose in the Missouri River just north of Stephen's Point."

Hood didn't recognize the voice. "Who is this?"

The sound of disconnection was affirmed by the phone display, which read: "Call ended." Hood shared the caller's warning with Wally, then added, "Let's check it out. I'll alert the state Water Patrol."

"Call Young John, too," Wally said. "Him and Art were scheduled for Ghoul Duty farther down river. We might need more than one boat to herd this thing. If it's one of those big commercial tanks and it's full, this could be a nightmare."

Hood placed the calls, then asked Wally: "How much time?"

"Depends," Wally said, his voice barely audible above the accelerated noise of the boat's motor. "If it's caught in the current, it'll take more time to close the gap."

"We can't let it hit the bridge."

"I know."

Hood's ringtone sounded.

"We see it," Young John's voice announced. "It's a big-ass tank."

"Where are you?" Hood asked.

"One-four-two mile marker, just downstream from Stephen's Point."

Hood relayed the information to Wally.

"Tell them we're on our way," Wally said. "A few minutes, max."

Hood repeated the information.

"Ask Young John if it's still moving or got snagged on something," Wally shouted.

Hood posed the question, then said, "It's still heading down river—fast."

"Damn," Wally said. He nudged the accelerator on the outboard. The motor labored and whined, but their speed increased.

Hood ended the call and clutched the sides of the boat. Tension twisted his neck muscles into knots. "How the hell does this happen, anyway? Those tanks are supposed to be strapped onto frames bolted to concrete pads."

"Flood could've weakened the straps or pried up the pad."

As the boat rounded a bend in the river, Hood scanned the surface of the water as it unfolded before him. "There it is," he shouted when the massive, 20,000-gallon propane tank came into view. It careened downstream like a wayward whale with the sunlight glinting from its silver surface. The boat operated by Young John kept pace beside it, and Wally maintained maximum speed until his craft closed the gap and flanked the propane tank on the opposite side.

"What's the plan?" Hood shouted. "Should we try to lasso it or something?"

"No," Wally said. "No way to hold it in this current. It'll just drag us along."

Hood remembered being towed by the uprooted tree and the peril they had faced just days before.

"What do you want us to do?" Young John yelled.

"There's a wing dam just below the one-three-four marker," Wally shouted back. "Maybe we can steer it into there."

"Steer it how?" Hood asked, clearly unnerved.

"We'll try to nudge it with the boats," Wally said.

Hood glared at him. "What if it's still got propane in it? We can't just ram into it."

"We'll need to be careful," Wally said.

"Careful," Hood shouted in an adrenaline-fueled panic. "What if we puncture it? What if a spark from the motor — ?"

"We can't just leave it out here," Wally said. "Sooner or later, it's gonna hit something — maybe the bridge supports."

Hood frowned. There was nothing about Wally's plan that he liked. But he didn't have a better one.

Wally continued relaying instructions to Young John until the wing dam appeared down river on the south bank. Wally maneuvered his boat ahead of where Young John's flanked the tank from the north. Hood braced himself against the bow as their boat bumped the propane tank, then winced as the tank received a more severe jolt from Young John's craft.

"Easy," Hood shouted, as the tank bobbed nearer the south bank, increasing its distance from them.

Wally angled into the tank and bumped it again, then accelerated slightly in an attempt to plow it toward the bank. Hood glanced downstream and saw the narrow arm of the wing dam extending into the river. The L-shaped configuration of the boulders protruded only slightly above the floodwaters.

Questions gushed into Hood's mind. Would Wally be able to guide the tank into the secure embrace of the dam? Would the rocks be stable enough to trap the tank, or would they collapse with the force of impact? Would the impending collision with the dam rupture the tank?

"Okay," Wally shouted to Young John. "Back off, back off now."

Hood watched the other boat decelerate as Wally continued pushing the giant tank. The boat's motor groaned with the strain. The tip of the wing dam loomed a hundred yards ahead, but the tank remained outside its protruding arm.

"We're not gonna make it," Hood shouted. Wally slowed the motor, and the boat backed off with a relieved idle. Hood relaxed for a brief moment before Wally gunned the motor and shouted: "Hang on!" In the instant the boat accelerated, Hood realized Wally had not conceded defeat. Hood gaped at his deputy, then at the propane tank as the boat rapidly closed the gap, swerved sharply, and broadsided the massive object.

The tank rammed into a boulder at the tip of the wing dam and wobbled momentarily, balanced precariously between settling into the safe embrace of the structure or washing back into the channel and continuing its headlong rush downstream. Wally worked furiously to spin the boat and pin the tank against the boulder, blocking any escape. The tank screeched against the rocks, triggering a small avalanche of stones sinking below the surface and creating a new opening.

"It's getting loose," Hood shouted.

Wally gunned the motor again and swept the boat in a tight circle. The tank groaned fitfully as the current held it precariously against the remaining rocks. Wally aimed the bow at the tank and sped forward. As he approached, he again veered sharply, smashing the hull broadside into the propane tank. The impact knocked Hood and Wally from their seats, and the unpiloted boat raced toward shore and ran aground, its prop churning up mud.

Wally scrambled back into his seat. "We did it," he shouted triumphantly. He cut the motor, then turned to his boss. "You okay?"

"I think so," Hood said. He sat, rubbed a bruised knee through torn trousers, and looked to where the propane tank bobbed serenely in the confines of the placid pool of water.

His smile twisted into a puzzled grimace as he spotted the words spray-painted sloppily on the side of the tank. It read: "Tick Tock."

He looked at Wally, who also was focused on the message.

"What the hell does that mean?" Wally asked in the same instant Hood realized he might know the answer.

Hood lingered at the office until Lester arrived for his evening shift. He watched his deputy get situated before summoning him. When Lester entered, Hood motioned for him to be seated, then closed his office door, a move that was not customary.

"I know what's going on," Hood said. He seated himself behind his desk.

"Yeah, Wally said you were onto us," Lester said. "It's just that after he told me about someone watching you and Elizabeth at the fair the other—"

"Relax. I didn't call you in here to discipline you."

Lester glanced at the closed door. "Okay?" he said, voicing it as a question.

"But if you guys insist on playing babysitter, you may as well keep your eyes open for Heath Schrock."

"Schrock? You think it might be Schrock?"

"Don't know," Hood said. That was true. He didn't know, but he suspected. Since he saw spray-painted message on the runaway propane tank, "Tick Tock" had been etched in his mind. He had made the connection to Schrock's nine-year-old comment when he was being led from the courtroom: "Your time will come, Francis. Tick tock." Although Hood had no proof and no evidence that the words on the tank were a threat from Schrock, he couldn't discount the possibility.

"So if I see Schrock," Lester said, "what do you want me to do?"

"Just let me know."

"Okay."

"Okay," Hood affirmed. As Lester rose to leave, the sheriff lifted his coffee cup, realized it was empty, and carried it to the coffee maker. As always, he glanced at Maggie's cup and asked if she wanted a refill.

"Just half," Maggie said.

When he finished pouring, he asked, "Do we still have a file on Heath Schrock?"

"If we do, it wouldn't be digital, it would be a paper file. I can check the ones we put in storage a few years ago."

Hood filled his own cup. "Sounds like a lot of trouble."

"It's not," Maggie said. "I cross-referenced them myself by name and date. What're you looking for?"

"Whatever background is available on Heath."

"I'll see what I can do."

Inside The Sportsmen's, Schrock sat on the same bar stool that had provoked his previous fight with Ansel Creighorn.

Lisa was preoccupied with other customers. She hurried to fill their orders, then approached Schrock. "Are you sure you should be here?" she asked. "The sheriff's been asking about you. And Creighorn's out. You showed him up. Nobody does that." She gestured to the ceiling damage caused by the shotgun blast. "Besides, I don't want the thought of an encore scaring off the customers. I need this job and these tips."

Schrock scanned the crowded interior. "Looks like it's more of an attraction."

"You watch your back." She turned to leave.

"Hold on." Schrock swiveled on his bar stool, turning full circle before facing her again. "Coast is clear," he said.

"Very funny," she said. She turned again to attend to other customers.

"Can I get a beer? Draw," Schrock called to her.

She drew the beer and placed the mug before him on a coaster.

"Thanks," he said. "Actually, I didn't come here to find Creighorn. I came to see you."

"What about?"

"What time do you finish tonight?"

"I'm closing, so not until two."

"I know this all-night restaurant. We could get a burger, maybe breakfast."

She shook her head. "Got to pick up Cody from his grandma's. Besides," she added, pointing to her wedding ring.

Schrock shrugged. "Just being friendly, is all."

"Thanks." She retreated.

Schrock exhaled a long breath, sipped his beer and watched Lisa as she tended the bar and filled drink orders. He was captivated by her graceful efficiency and economy of movement—qualities he considered uniquely female. His attitudes and actions toward men and women differed, he knew. He disliked most other men and was wary of their motives, and not only because he had witnessed and endured brutality while in prison. From an early age—beginning with his father and, later, his schoolmates—his experiences with men were rooted in conflict, dominance, and degradation.

Not so with women. His memories of his mother were enveloped in compassion, kindness, and love. Men were unworthy and undeserving of the adoration Schrock reserved for women. His musings vanished as he sensed someone approaching from behind. Schrock turned quickly and alertly, prepared to defend himself, then relaxed at the sight of a scrawny man he recognized from the other night as one of Creighorn's fellow pool players.

"You Heath?" the man asked.

"Who's asking?"

"Name's Herman Wallendorf. I remember you from school at R-1. You were a couple years behind me."

"You say Wallendorf?"

"Yeah."

"You related to that deputy?"

"Yeah. I'm his kid brother."

A brief silence ensued until Schrock said, "So what do you want?"

"Don't want nothing." He leaned closer and whispered. "You didn't hear this from me, but Ansel Creighorn's sitting in his truck in the parking lot. His arm's in a sling but he's got a gun."

"Why you telling me?"

"I don't want Ansel doing something stupid—again. Plus, nobody deserves getting ambushed in a parking lot."

Schrock studied the man momentarily. "Thanks."

"Remember, you didn't hear it from me."

After Herman went back to the poolroom, Schrock finished his beer and signaled Lisa.

"Another?" she asked.

He motioned her closer, then whispered, "That guy shooting pool just tipped me off that Creighorn's waiting for me outside. I don't know whether it's a heads up or part of a setup."

Lisa looked into the poolroom, where Herman and Neil Bowden were engaged in a game. "Which one?" she asked.

"Said his name's Herman."

"If it was Neil, I'd say it's a setup. With Herman, I dunno."

"There a back door?"

"Down the hallway past the restrooms."

"Thanks."

"Careful," Lisa warned as Schrock stood and headed toward the back door.

When he was gone, Herman skulked to a window overlooking the parking lot and watched.

Outside, Schrock slithered around the side of the building and stopped when he spotted the white pickup with Creighorn Excavating Co. displayed on the door. As Herman had warned, Creighorn was sitting behind the wheel watching the entrance. Schrock opened the blade of a large, lock-back knife he carried, stooped low, and crept stealthily among the parked vehicles. He approached Creighorn's truck from the rear and knelt just behind the driver's door. Schrock listened to the seamless hum of cicadas permeating the evening stillness, punctuated by the unmistakable sound of a push against the dashboard cigarette lighter. When he heard the lighter spring back, Schrock popped up from his crouch. He reached both hands through the open window, pinning Creighorn's right wrist against the steering wheel and pressing the knife blade against the big man's throat.

"If you so much as twitch," Schrock said, "I'll cut you wide open."

Creighorn remained still, the unlit cigarette pinched between his lips, his left arm immobilized by the sling, his secured right hand still reaching for the lighter, and a black handgun lying in his lap.

"Put that hand on the dash," Schrock ordered, "and don't get smart going for the lighter."

He released the man's wrist and Creighorn obeyed. Schrock reached down, took the gun, and tucked it into his own waistband. Then he reached into the cab and removed Ansel's key ring from the ignition. The ring contained a dozen or so keys and a metal fob in the shape of a skull.

"Those are my fuckin' keys," Creighorn complained.

"Let me tell you something," Schrock said. "If I see you again, I'll shoot you in the face with your own gun. Understood?"

Creighorn said nothing.

Schrock pressed the knife blade until a rivulet of blood ran down Creighorn's neck. "Understood?"

"Yeah," Creighorn spat.

"Good." Schrock removed the knife from Creighorn's throat and pocketed the key ring. He lingered long enough to puncture both driver's-side tires on the truck, then left.

CHAPTER
13

Tick, tock.

The words reverberated in the sheriff's mind as he placed a manila folder and his morning coffee on his desk.

As promised, Maggie had retrieved Heath Schrock's file. When she had handed it to her boss, she said, "There wasn't much background in it, so I took the liberty of getting a copy of the pre-sentence investigation on Heath. It's in the back."

Hood found the pre-sentence report and perused the biographical information. He learned Heath was an only child, son of Robert and Mae Ellen Schrock, 104 Old Sawmill Road. He attended Huhman County R-1 schools. When he was age 12, his mother drowned in the Missouri River. No determination could be made whether it was accident or suicide; the cause of death was listed as inconclusive. Thereafter, Heath continued to live with his father, with two exceptions. The boy stayed with an aunt and uncle during the six-month period while his father served a jail sentence. Later, he became a ward of the state for a shorter period of time after a teacher reported evidence consistent with physical abuse and the Missouri Division of Children's Services intervened. At age 15, after completion of his freshman year, he was charged with felony assault for shooting Sheriff Cliff Westerman. Heath was certified to stand trial as an adult, and he pleaded guilty in Huhman County Circuit Court.

Hood flipped to the comments page, where some relatives and educators described Heath as "withdrawn" or "introspective." One teacher wrote, "Heath can be confrontational with other boys, but he treats the girls with courtesy and respect that borders on reverence."

The report filled in some blanks, but Hood wanted more. He picked up the receiver of his desk phone and called Dr. Lawrence Gregory, a psychologist at the Missouri State Hospital, operated by the state's Department of Mental Health. The sheriff had consulted with Gregory on past cases. He appreciated the doctor's professionalism, candor, and ability to translate complex terminology into laymen's language. He listened to the automated options and keyed in the doctor's extension. Expecting he would leave a message on voice mail, he was startled to hear Gregory's live greeting. They exchanged brief pleasantries before Hood said, "I know you're busy and I don't want to take up too much of your time, but I've been wondering. If I wanted to get information—you know, like a psychological profile—on an ex-con, would the authorities be able to give it to me?"

"Is this someone we treated?"

"No. He was in a Department of Corrections facility."

"I'm no expert on their policies," Gregory said. "We're under Mental Health, not Corrections."

"I know. I was just wondering."

"The short answer is: it depends," Gregory said. "Is this

connected with a crime that's been committed or you believe is about to be committed?"

"Let me tell you why I'm asking," Hood said. He described the release of Heath Schrock, the mysterious appearance of the black truck, the vanishing watcher at the county fair, the runaway propane tank, and the graffiti on its side. "So," he concluded, "that's why I'm interested in getting Schrock's profile, either from his doctor or his records."

"You're probably not going to like this answer, Francis," Gregory said, "but if you asked me for a patient's information based on what you just said, I would decline. There are situations that override doctor-patient confidentiality, but they would need to involve a threat by the patient to harm himself or someone else. At this juncture, you may have an implied threat based on a potential grudge, but it also may be your own imagination or interpretation. By your own admission, you haven't identified this person as the source of a threat. In my book, there's not enough to trump doctor-patient confidentiality, not at this time."

"I figured as much. I wanted to ask you because I knew you'd give a straight answer, keep me from making an ass of myself."

"I appreciate the compliment, but may I give you some advice?"

"Sure."

"That convenience store—the one where you saw the truck—do you stop there regularly?"

Hood was expecting a statement, not a question. "Pretty much every morning," he said.

"It's always advisable for people in authority, particularly law enforcement, to avoid patterned behavior. That may explain the truck if it was left there purposely. Your Mr. — what was it — Schnack?"

"Schrock."

"Right. All he'd have to do is watch you for a few days to know your routine."

"But I like their coffee," Hood said.

"You're incorrigible, Francis, but consider the advice." After a momentary silence, he added, "And one more thing — trust your instincts. If you're feeling uneasy, there's probably a reason."

"Thanks," Hood said.

He disconnected, and almost immediately, Wally appeared in the doorframe, accompanied by his brother Herman. "I thought you needed to hear this right away," Wally said to his boss. "Can I close this?" he added, gesturing to the door. Hood nodded. He sensed the seriousness in his deputy's demeanor and invited the brothers to sit.

"Herman," Wally said, "tell the sheriff what you just told me."

Herman squirmed with obvious nervousness, then blurted: "Creighorn said I done it, but I don't know, sheriff. I don't remember."

Hood's expression reflected his confusion.

"Whoa," Wally advised his brother before Hood could

speak. "Slow down, start from the beginning, and repeat what you just told me."

"Okay," Herman said. He inhaled a long breath. "We were drinking at The Sportsmen's—"

"This was back in April, right?" Wally asked.

"Yeah, sometime in April. It was after work, a Thursday, I think. A bunch of us were drinking and shooting pool and just hanging out, you know." He paused and inhaled another breath. "And next thing we know, it's closing time. Well, some of us weren't done yet; we still had some drinking to do. So we piled in Creighorn's truck and mine and—"

"Who's we?" Hood asked.

"Well, Neil—Neil Bowden—he was in Creighorn's truck, and Travis was with me."

"Travis Haulenbach?" Hood said.

"Yeah. So we drive out to the cemetery—it's quiet—"

"Our Lady of Help?" Hood asked. "Where you work?"

"Yeah. We've done it before. Like I was saying, it's quiet and by the river and nobody hassles us. So we're sitting around on the tailgates drinking and horsing around, and that's the last thing I remember about that night. But the next day, Travis didn't show up for work. I figured he was hung over big time; I know I was. Then he missed work again, and I was at The Sportsmen's bitching about Travis not showing up, and Creighorn pulled me aside. He asked if I remembered what happened and I said 'no,' and he said don't you remember arguing with Travis and whacking him with a shovel?"

Hood's lips tightened in consternation. "You hit him with a shovel? Then what?"

"Don't know," Herman said, beginning to lose his composure. "I never saw him again. After what Creighorn said, I went back and looked all around the cemetery and the bottomlands there. No Travis."

"Why didn't you report it?" Hood asked.

"I didn't know what to do. I figured if I did hit him like Creighorn said, I must've just knocked him out. I figured he got up later and was pissed off, decided he wasn't gonna work with me no more, and left town."

"Until we found his body," Hood said.

"Yeah. When you guys came out to the church and showed me that picture and told me he was dead, I—" Herman stopped abruptly, his voice wracked with a half-coughing, half-choking sound. Wally put a supportive hand on his brother's shoulder.

"Need some water?" Hood asked.

"Yeah."

Hood fetched the water himself, giving the brothers a few moments together. When he returned, Herman appeared to have regained some composure.

"Just a few more questions," Hood said. He returned to his seat. "What were you arguing with Travis about?"

"I don't remember, but it was probably money. He owed me a hundred bucks. He kept putting me off."

"How'd you get home that night?"

"Don't know. I woke up in my apartment, and my truck

was parked outside, so I guess I drove home, but I don't remember doing it."

Hood guessed Herman had suffered a blackout— something he himself had experienced prior to recovery. He would awaken with no memory of the score of the baseball game he was watching or even what he had eaten for supper. Although his episodes had occurred at home, he was aware of how complete, and frightening, the memory loss could be.

"Maybe," Wally said, "Neil drove you home in your truck, then hitched a ride with Creighorn."

"Maybe," Herman conceded, "but if I accidentally killed Travis, driving drunk is the least of my problems."

"Let's just stick to what you know," Hood said. "Speaking of Neil, did he say anything about what happened? Did he see you hit Travis with a shovel?"

"Never said. I don't know if he saw anything. Later, at The Sportsmen's, Creighorn was teasing him about being a lightweight and falling asleep in the cab of the truck."

"What happened to the shovel?" Hood asked.

Herman shrugged. "Don't know that, either. There's a couple in the bed of my truck, though."

Hood looked from Herman to Wally, who seemed dumbfounded. "Herman," Hood said, "I need to confer with your brother for a few minutes. I'm going to have somebody come sit with you. Okay?"

"I guess I'm in big trouble, huh?" Herman asked.

"We just need to sort this out," Hood said. "We'll be back in a few minutes."

After Hood and Wally left the office, the sheriff motioned for Young John. Hood briefed his rookie deputy on the situation and instructed him to sit with Herman and make sure he didn't try to leave or make any phone calls. Hood then led Wally to an unpopulated corner where a bank of windows looked out on the parking lot.

"You realize I'll need to call in some help on this one," Hood said. "I hate to say it, but I'll have to ask Sauers to assemble a task force. I can't allow the sheriff's department to be the sole agency investigating a case involving my chief deputy's brother. There's too much appearance of a conflict-of-interest. Plus, we'll need some trained interviewers and forensic experts on the team."

Wally nodded.

"I plan to stay involved," Hood continued, "but you'll need to distance yourself—completely." His tone had switched from co-worker to commander. "And I mean starting now."

"I understand," Wally said, his agreement tinged with reluctance.

"Okay," Hood said. "You head back to your desk. I'll keep you posted."

After they separated, Hood returned to his office. He motioned for Young John to stay. "Herman," he said, "we need to investigate what you've told us. You understand?"

Herman nodded.

"Your cooperation would be helpful. Can I count on that?"

"Uh huh."

"First, we're going to need your fingerprints. And we'll need to impound your truck and its contents."

"Why?"

"Evidence," Hood said. "You say you have no memory of what happened. All you know is what Ansel Creighorn told you. We need to examine the truck and tools to see if they tell us anything."

"But I need those for work."

"I understand. We'll try to get them back to you as quickly as possible."

"Are you gonna talk to Creighorn?

"As quickly as I can," Hood said. "And Neil, too."

Herman hesitated. "So what d'ya want me to do? Am I under arrest?"

"No," Hood said. "In fact, John will drive you back to your place. But for the time being, until you hear from me, I want you to stay away from Creighorn and Neil—no phone calls, no hanging out at The Sportsmen's, no nothing. Will you do that?"

Herman nodded.

After Herman and Young John left, the sheriff reviewed Herman's story, which answered some questions but raised others. He reached for his phone to call Sauers, but hesitated. Sauers, Hood suspected, would try to take charge of the case. Hood's impulse was to conjure some deft illusion whereby he would seem to yield control to Sauers, but continue to orchestrate the investigation. He dismissed the idea. His program of recovery, he reminded himself, was based on honesty and openness. Controlling, self-centered behaviors were hallmarks of his former self, not his sober self. He placed the call and briefed the police lieutenant on the situation.

"I understand the conflict of interest," Sauers said. "It's also a cold case, which doesn't help."

"Agreed," Hood said. "Mostly, what we need are some people to interview Ansel Creighorn and Neil Bowden separately, but as simultaneously as possible so they don't have a chance to compare stories."

"So what are we looking at—four, five people?"

"Sounds right." Hood said.

"Anybody in particular you want on the team?"

Hood was pleasantly surprised by the question. "Be good to have somebody from the crime lab since we'll need to have Herman's truck—and Creighorn's, too—processed. If she's available, my first choice would be Sandra Brondel," Hood said, referring to one of the lab's veteran forensic specialists.

"Let me see what I can do," Sauers said.

"Probation and Parole. Janelle speaking."

"Hi, Janelle," Hood greeted. "This is your sheriff."

"Hi, Francis. Who messed up this time?" she asked, her resignation apparent.

"Can't I just call to say 'hi?'"

"You can, but you never do."

"Actually, I'm not calling to report an arrest or violation. I need some information."

"Shoot."

"I saw on the Corrections paperwork that Heath Schrock was assigned to you. I wanted to know if he's behaving."

"He's been a regular altar boy," Janelle said. "Makes every appointment, on time, has a place to stay, works part time."

"Sounds almost too good to be true."

"Might be, but I haven't had time to check on him yet. You know how it is—understaffed, overworked, ankle-deep in paperwork. Plus the violators get all the attention, which is the way it has to be."

"I hear you," Hood said, commiserating.

"So, for right now, I'm trusting him."

"Where's he living?"

"Hold on. Let me call up his file."

Hood heard the faint tapping of keystrokes. "He's staying with his cousin, Ronnie, over on Alcorn, number 406," Janelle said. "It's the low-rent district, I know, but hey—" she left the remainder of the sentence unfinished.

"And his job?"

"I don't know if he's started yet, but Heath said his cousin offered to pay him if he helps out. Ronnie does odd jobs—mows lawns, does some carpentry, hauls stuff away, that sort of thing."

"Interesting," Hood said, a word he used when he had nothing to say.

Silence gathered momentarily before Janelle said, "I've really been meaning to pay him a visit, check on things. Want me to move him to the top of my priority list?"

"No need," Hood said.

"Can I ask — is there a reason for your interest?"

"Call it curiosity."

"You know what they say about curiosity, Francis."

"I do," he answered. "Thanks, Janelle."

Hood watched the clock, which signaled 5:06 p.m. Before he entered recovery, he had resolved never to take a drink before 5 p.m., even on weekends. He figured if he could control his drinking, he wasn't an alcoholic. When he had admitted he was an alcoholic, he adopted a new routine to remain on the job until 5:30 p.m., which would give him at least a half-hour head start on an evening of abstinence.

He took his newspapers to the recycle box Maggie had created. When he returned and looked at the clock, the time was 5:13. He picked a Styrofoam cup out of the trash basket and carefully began peeling it like an orange, starting from the top. A prisoner who had spent 30 days of shock detention in the county jail had perfected the technique, leaving a long curlicue of Styrofoam in his cell every day. One day Hood decided to watch him on the monitor. The prisoner's concentration and patience were mesmerizing. Not until Maggie interrupted did Hood realize he had been watching for nearly 20 minutes. Before Hood completed peeling the first circular layer, the Styrofoam broke, leaving little white bits on his fingers. He looked at the clock — 5:21. Close enough, he decided. He dropped the damaged cup back in the trash and, as he arose from his chair, his telephone rang.

The caller was Lieutenant Sauers. Hood sat back down.

"There's four of us, counting you, who can split into pairs and interview your guys tomorrow morning if you can find out where they'll be."

"Great," Hood said.

"Sandra is available," Sauers continued, "but she's not comfortable with interrogation, so I'm inclined to pair her with Tim Johnson, who said he'd help."

"Good," Hood said. Johnson, a Highway Patrol captain, was a seasoned investigator.

"I figured you and I could take the other guy," Sauers said. "Now we just need to decide which team gets which guy."

Hood had a preference, but wasn't sure if Sauers would be cooperative or contrary. "I'd really like to hear what Creighorn has to say," he said.

"Creighorn it is," Sauers agreed.

CHAPTER
14

Activity had resumed at the construction site following a dormant period dictated by heavy rains. The rapping from nail guns and hammers established an erratic percussion blended with the rhythmic drone of power saws.

Hood and Sauers continued past the wooden skeletons of what would become moderately priced homes and surveyed the deforested acreage where excavating equipment navigated an invisible, seemingly random pattern. They spotted Ansel Creighorn shouting instructions to a bulldozer operator. As the uniformed duo approached, the dozer operator pointed to them, informing his boss of their presence.

Creighorn turned and walked toward them. The giant's long, black curls protruded wildly from a yellow hard hat, and his left arm remained immobilized by a sling. "This is a hard-hat area," he barked.

"Then you'll need to come with us," Sauers said.

"Him I know," Creighorn said, indicating the sheriff. "Who are you?"

"Police Lieutenant Gene Sauers." He displayed his shield.

"Already talked to the sheriff about that thing at The Sportsmen's," Creighorn said. "Even spent the night—"

"This isn't about that," Sauers said. "We're investigating the death of Travis Haulenbach."

Although Creighorn made no immediate reply, Hood noticed the big man's swagger fade. "Maybe I ought to call my lawyer," Creighorn said.

"That's up to you," Sauers replied. "We were hoping you could tell us what you saw."

"Saw?"

"The night you, Travis, Herman Wallendorf, and Neil Bowden went out drinking together in April at Our Lady of Help Cemetery."

"What makes you think I know anything about that?"

"I'll ask the questions, Mr. Creighorn," Sauers said. "Let's just say we have information—"

"Fuckin' Herman," Creighorn muttered. He looked at Hood. "Or was it Neil?"

"We're going to need a statement," Sauers said, his tone officious.

"I'm on the job."

"And we're investigating a possible homicide," Sauers countered. "You'll need to come with us."

"I'm calling my lawyer first."

"That's your prerogative, Mr. Creighorn, but we're not charging you with a crime."

"Then why do I need to go to the station? Right now?"

"You don't if you cooperate and tell us what you witnessed."

"I'm not saying shit without my lawyer."

"Then you leave us no choice," Sauers said. "You have the right to remain—"

"You said you weren't arresting me. What's going on?"

"You're a material witness in a possible homicide investigation. Withholding evidence is obstruction of justice. I suspect a judge will be happy to issue a warrant to that effect. In the meantime, we can hold you for twenty hours."

"You're fucking kidding me," Creighorn said, his voice rising.

"And we'll need to impound your truck—and its contents."

"Good luck with that," Creighorn said. "It's sitting on a jack stand in The Sportsmen's parking lot. I got one of my ex's cars today. Used it to drop off two punctured tires to be patched."

"And we'll need the truck keys."

"Lost 'em," Creighorn said. "But there's a spare set stashed in the truck's engine compartment—by the wiper fluid reservoir."

Hood considered the new information—two punctured tires and "lost" keys—and couldn't help but wonder if Creighorn's run of bad luck was too much of a coincidence.

Hood and Sauers entered the interview room and sat across the table from where Creighorn's lawyer Albert Vanderfeltz had conferred confidentially with his client.

"We'll be recording this interview," Sauers said. "Any objections?"

"Nope," Creighorn said, pre-empting his lawyer. "My attorney said if I tell you guys what happened, I got nothin' to worry about."

"What were you worried about?" Sauers asked.

"You know, that 'accessory' shit," Creighorn said.

"After hearing my client's narrative," Vanderfeltz said, "I'm sure you'll agree he was not an accessory before or after the fact. He simply witnessed an assault—an assault, I might add, that was never reported by the victim or assailant."

"That's because one's dead and the other can't remember," Hood muttered.

His interjection prompted a momentary glare from Sauers before the lieutenant again faced Creighorn and said, "Just tell us what you observed."

Creighorn's account began much like Herman had described. Hood listened for differences, leaning slightly forward when Creighorn elaborated on Herman's story or provided new information.

"So we're out there drinking and shooting the shit," Creighorn said, "and Herman and Travis start getting into it."

"What about?" Sauers asked.

"Money. Seems Herman loaned Travis some money, which I guess he pissed away and couldn't pay back. They started arguing and the next thing I know Herman is holding a shovel and whacks Travis upside the head."

"You're saying you witnessed Herman Wallendorf assault Travis Haulenbach with a shovel and deliver a blow to the head?"

"Yeah, and Travis goes down like a sack of shit, and I'm thinking, 'What the fuck?' So I figure I don't need this and get in my truck and take off."

"Where was Neil during all this?" Hood asked, indifferent to Sauers' reaction.

"Asleep in the cab of my truck. He slept through the whole fucking thing. Didn't wake up 'til I dropped him at his place."

"What about Herman?"

Creighorn shrugged. "I just left. I don't know what Herman did. Guess he drove home."

"So you just left Travis lying there on the ground?"

"Yeah." Creighorn looked down at his hands, which were folded and resting on the table. "Look, I ain't proud of that, but I was pretty wasted and things were going south. I just wanted to get the fuck out of there."

"Did you think Travis Haulenbach was dead?" Sauers asked.

"No. I didn't know until you guys told me. I figured when Herman said he wasn't still laying out there, Travis must've got up at some point and took off." Creighorn paused. "I don't think I'd stay around after my boss hit me with a fucking shovel."

When the four task-force members convened to compare notes after their respective interviews, they determined Creighorn and Neil largely had corroborated each other's story. Neil had not requested an attorney and said he had fallen asleep in the cab of Creighorn's pickup not long after the drinking session moved to the cemetery. He said he had heard only later—during a conversation with Creighorn— that Herman had knocked out Travis, who presumably had regained consciousness at some point and left town.

After conferring, the task force members discussed what they knew and what remained inconclusive. Creighorn's eyewitness account was sufficient to seek an assault charge— but not a murder charge—against Herman. Travis's death likely was caused by the shovel blow to the head delivered by a drunken Herman, but likelihood was not proof. The task force members decided to await crime lab analyses of the pickup trucks and their contents, in hopes the physical evidence would provide greater clarity.

Hood parked his cruiser in his designated space at the courthouse. As he got out, he saw an attractive woman approaching. She held her hand to her face in a futile attempt to conceal swelling and bruising below her left eye. Although he hadn't seen her in person for decades, he recognized her from photos in newspaper ads and on billboards.

"Francis," she said, her expression and tone revealing agitation.

"Cheryl." He wondered if saying no more than her name masked his surprise and confusion.

"Can I talk to you?"

"Of course." Hood briefly evaluated her condition. The facial bruise and reddened eyes were the only indicators something was amiss. He guessed Cheryl had been crying, but had restored her makeup and hairstyle to flawless condition. He also noticed her insistence on smoothing any rumpling of her floral blouse and pleated skirt. Her demeanor reminded him of her capacity for making the best of a bad situation. "Are you all right?"

"I'm fine. It's about my husband. He's in your jail. They won't let me see him."

"Let's go to my office. We can talk there."

Hood escorted Cheryl inside, stopping briefly to ask Maggie for the incident report connected to David Grimm's arrest. When she told him responding deputy Lester Stackhouse had not filed the report yet, Hood walked Cheryl to his office. He gestured to the visitors' chairs facing his desk and invited her to sit.

"It's all just a misunderstanding," she said. She remained standing. "I need to see him."

"Please," Hood said, "sit for a minute." He intentionally sat in one of the visitors' chairs and waited until she followed his lead. "I'm at a disadvantage here. I've been out of the office, and the incident report hasn't been filed yet. Why don't you tell me what happened?"

"I went out for a drink after work with Gwen, one of my co-workers. She's a mother, a little younger than me, and her teenager has been giving her fits. I remember what that's like, so I thought she could use some talk therapy. Anyway, we were—"

"Where was this?"

"Stoney Creek Winery. It's off Route DD just outside of—"

"I know it," Hood said. "Haven't been there for a while, but it's a nice place. Go on."

"Anyway, we were talking and drinking wine and— who should show up?—our boss. So, we had to invite him to sit with us—what else could we do? We were just chatting and laughing—not even work stuff—and my husband walked in. You know David, right? Of course you do. I had sent him a text from work to tell him where I was going and what I was doing, but I guess he expected me home sooner."

Cheryl smoothed her skirt, again, then looked down at the floor. "It's my fault. I lost track of time. I was on my second or third glass of wine, and I was getting a little tipsy." She looked up, into Hood's eyes. "I think David had been drinking, too. He said some ugly things—to me, to Gwen, to my boss. David has—it's like he has this line and, once he crosses it, I can't reach him. I tried to explain, to apologize, but I knew he was over the line. I thought maybe if I just left, he would follow me out, but . . ." She released a single sob, leaving the sentence incomplete.

Hood waited while she struggled to regain control.

"He slapped me," she continued. "He called me a 'slut' and he hit me. Here," she pointed to her bruised cheek, which continued to swell. She laughed briefly, a reaction that surprised

Hood, then seemed to withdraw into her own thoughts. "I don't know which was worse — the slur or the slap." She seemed to teeter on the brink of losing composure again, then stiffened and asked, "Can I use your ladies' room?"

"Sure." He directed her to the restroom, then waited.

The woman who returned seemed transformed. Although her appearance was largely unchanged, her attitude and approach were all business. "What happens next?" she asked, as she resumed her seat.

"That depends. The responding deputy will file a report, which will be forwarded to the prosecutor, who will decide what criminal charges to file, if any."

"I don't intend to file charges."

Hood spread his hands. "That may be a factor, but the incident happened in a public place. There were witnesses. It's really up to the prosecutor — "

"Couldn't you just let it go? I mean, you decide what reports go to the prosecutor, right? You could just give David a warning, turn him loose."

Hood had fielded this question before. "It's, um, too far along for that." He adopted his explanatory, apologetic tone. "The incident report's being completed, David's been arrested and processed as a jail inmate. The next step in the process — "

"But you're the one who takes the next step. I've known you since middle school, Francis. We're friends, we dated in high school. Couldn't you overlook this, for me?"

Hood looked away. He was silent.

"You are so straight-laced, so by-the-book — always have been, even in high school."

When Hood didn't answer, she shifted in an attempt to move into his field of vision. "This is personal, isn't it?" she challenged. "It's because of David, because of what he did to you?"

Hood faced her. He wasn't sure how to answer.

"Or is it because of me?" Cheryl added. "Because I went with him, because I chose him?"

The incident, the second-guessing, the could haves, the should haves fast-forwarded in his mind. He remembered what his recovery sponsor had said about examining his motives. He said nothing.

"Can I at least see him?" Cheryl asked.

"Yes," Hood answered. He phoned one of his jailers to make arrangements, then escorted Cheryl to the connecting portal, unlocked the steel door, and introduced her to the jailer.

After she stepped through the portal, she turned and faced Hood, who remained where he was. "Are you coming, too?" she asked.

"No." He closed and sealed the door.

CHAPTER
15

Herman Wallendorf pushed a stake into the spongy turf of the relatively flat, grassy area that served as the site of the annual Our Lady of Help parish picnic. He wiggled the stake, pulled the cord connected to the top of the volleyball net to tighten the tension, then wrapped it around the peg. If the rains held off, as predicted, he guessed the event would proceed as planned. Either way, lining lanes for the sack race and planting croquet wickets was a welcome respite from the laborious task of clearing ground for the new cemetery. He picked up another stake, straightened, and saw a battered black pickup truck parked in the lot. He watched as Heath Schrock emerged from the interior and approached.

"Heath, what brings you out here?" Herman said, holding both a stake and mallet, as if ready to battle a vampire.

"So this is where you work, huh?"

"Yeah. How'd you find me?"

"Wasn't hard."

"So what's going on?"

"I wanted to say thanks for the heads up the other night."

"Yeah, well, no problem. I just don't want it to get back to Ansel that I tipped you off."

"Don't worry," Schrock said. "He's plenty pissed at me, though. I took his gun and his keys, then punctured a couple tires."

"Yeah. I saw his truck in the parking lot when I left," Herman said, making no mention he had watched the incident from the poolroom.

"I don't wanna keep you from your work." Schrock surveyed the area as if baffled by the wire wickets sprouting from the freshly mown grass.

"Parish picnic tomorrow," Herman said. "If it don't get rained out."

Schrock nodded. "What's the deal with this Creighorn guy? Does he know when to quit, or what?"

"He can carry a grudge."

"That's what I figured. So I should watch my back, right?"

Herman nodded.

Schrock reached in his pocket and removed a key ring. "Well, you may as well give him these." He extended Creighorn's recognizable ring with its metal skull fob.

Herman took them, but said nothing.

Schrock glanced skyward, followed by Herman, as if both men were trying to interpret the darkening clouds collecting in an otherwise blue sky.

"You been a regular at The Sportsmen's for a while, right?" Schrock asked, breaking the shared silence.

"A while."

"What's the story with Lisa, the barmaid?"

"How do you mean?" Herman replied, sensing the question was the real reason for Schrock's visit.

"I dunno. She seems to run hot and cold."

"She gets hit on a lot. I mean, I can see how it's her job to be friendly, but she's a fox and she's around guys who are drinking and think they're God's gift, so that shit's gotta get old. Plus, she's married and has a kid. Her husband's doing time, but from what I can tell she ain't looking for substitutes." A lone raindrop struck his scalp. "Why?"

"Just asking."

"Okay," Herman said, without conviction.

"No, I mean, what you said makes sense. I know Buddy from doing time, so when Lisa and I got talking, she seemed, like, interested, but then these walls went up and—I dunno."

"Women," Herman said, as if the word contained a definitive explanation.

As anticipated, dots of rain sprinkled their faces and arms.

"Shit," Herman muttered. "Better get these tools in."

"I gotta go, anyway," Schrock said. "See you around."

"Yeah, sure."

Wally stood inside the door of The Sportsmen's and scanned the interior looking for his brother. Herman was nowhere to be seen. Wally focused instead on Ansel Creighorn and Neil Bowden, who were throwing darts in a corner the main bar room. Wally was hoping to talk with his younger brother—who had not answered or returned his phone calls—to see how he was coping. Although Wally was keenly aware of the instructions to steer clear of the Haulenbach investigation, he approached the two men.

Creighorn ignored the deputy and concentrated on lining up his next throw. Neil manufactured a surly expression as he stared at the deputy.

"Looking for my brother," Wally said.

Creighorn launched the dart, seemingly satisfied with his toss. "Ain't seen 'im," he said, as he plucked another from within the sling immobilizing his left arm.

"Tonight or lately?"

Creighorn looked up. "Most people know better than to annoy me when I'm playing darts."

"I'm not most people."

Creighorn turned to Wally, seemingly sizing him up. "Not tonight and not lately," he said. "In fact, not since he went crying to the sheriff about what he done."

"You have something to say about that?"

"Not to you. Already talked to your boss and some cop," Creighorn said. "Ask them."

Wally faced Neil. "What about you, Neil?"

"I—" Neil began.

"Neil didn't see nothin'," Creighorn interrupted, his tone emphatic. "Neil didn't hear nothin', and Neil don't know nothin'. Ain't that right, Neil?"

Neil nodded dutifully.

"So, that's it?" Wally asked.

"That's it, except tell your boss to hurry the fuck up so I can get my truck back." Creighorn launched another dart. "Besides, when I saw Hood with the cop, I figured he took you off the case because of your brother. Are you even supposed to be here asking us questions?"

"I'm off duty, just looking for Herman."

"Maybe I should tell your boss you came around off duty and started hassling us with a bunch of questions. How would that be?"

Wally shrugged, feigning nonchalance, although he knew Creighorn's threat could be a problem.

"Anything else?" Creighorn asked, then added, "Deputy."

"No," Wally answered. He turned and left.

Several hours and pitchers of beer later, Creighorn was again throwing darts when Herman entered The Sportsmen's. Herman was surprised to see Creighorn, who staggered to the dartboard and retrieved the projectiles. Herman was considering retreat when Creighorn turned, noticed him, and hollered, "Herman."

"Hey, Ansel," Herman greeted. "Didn't know you were here. Didn't see your truck outside."

"Neil gave me a ride. Sheriff took my truck. You wouldn't know—"

"Where is Neil?" Herman asked, scanning the interior.

"Tapping a kidney, I guess. You wouldn't know anything about that, would you?"

"About Neil?"

"' Bout my truck?"

"Well, after the sheriff and my brother pulled the body of that guy I worked with—that Travis guy—out of the river, I told them about the thing this spring when we all got drunk and you told me I hit Travis with the shovel."

"What d'ya want to do a thing like that for?"

"I felt bad. I mean, I thought I just knocked him cold. I didn't think I killed him. When I went back to check on him, he was gone."

"Well, they took my fuckin' truck."

"You'll get it back in a day or so. They took mine, too, if it means anything."

"Don't mean shit to me," Creighorn said. He stepped to the line, swayed momentarily and squinted at the dartboard, preparing his next toss.

"Be right back," Herman said, seizing the opportunity to walk into the empty poolroom. He fingered Creighorn's key ring, hidden in his pocket. His intention was to leave it on the pool table rail, to be found and ultimately returned to its owner. Herman had no intention of handing it directly to Creighorn and face questions about how he had obtained the ring taken by Schrock.

As Herman laid the key ring on the pool table rail, Neil's familiar voice called, "Hey, Herman, what's going on?"

Herman turned, purposely using his body to obstruct Neil's view of the key ring. "Not much," he answered. "Just stopped by for a few minutes."

Neil approached. "I'm gonna buy us another pitcher. Why don't you stay and, hey—" he said, looking past Herman and noticing the key ring, "are those Ansel's keys?"

Herman stepped closer to Neil so he could whisper. "Yeah, but do me a favor, okay? Don't tell Ansel I put 'em there. He'll just ask a bunch of questions about how I got 'em. Somebody'll see 'em sitting on the rail soon enough."

"Okay, but how'd you get 'em?"

"The short answer is Heath Schrock gave 'em to me to give back to Ansel," Herman said

"So the guy Ansel tangled with was Heath Schrock?"

"Yeah, but Ansel doesn't need to know that, either. At least, not from one of us. Bringing it up will just piss him off and you know what that's like."

"'Yeah. Sure you won't stay and have a beer with us?"

"Can't," Herman said. "Gotta go."

"Okay," Neil repeated.

Herman took out his wallet, removed a ten-dollar bill and handed it to Neil. "Next pitcher's on me," he said. "And thanks, man."

"Sure," Neil said.

CHAPTER
16

Ann.

The name sounded in Hood's mind as he stood before the bathroom sink, lathering the morning stubble on his face. He mentally massaged the inexact name until it yielded Anna.

He stroked his cheek with the razor.

Ann. Anna.

Still not right. He rinsed the razor, shaved his chin.

Anna something.

Warmer. He rinsed the blade again, watched lather and whiskers circle the drain.

Something Anna. Mary Ann.

Almost. He lifted his chin and stroked his throat.

Maryland.

That's it. The synapse connected in the instant before his hand flinched. He saw the first drop of blood disperse as it hit the white porcelain of the sink basin. "Damn," he muttered as he put down the razor and applied pressure to the cut. Why, he wondered, had he not made the connection before? He was reminded of one of those hidden-object drawings that, once solved, seems so obvious.

Both Travis Haulenbach and Ansel Creighorn had lived in Maryland.

Maintaining pressure on the cut, he left the bathroom and retrieved his cell phone as questions tumbled in his mind. He recalled Herman telling him Haulenbach and Creighorn sometimes would share recollections of "old times." Was Annapolis, Haulenbach's former residence, the city where the two men connected? How old were they at the time? Did Haulenbach deliberately track down Creighorn in central Missouri? If so, why? Or, he considered, was it merely coincidence that the two men ended up in the same Missouri county, halfway across the country?

He called Maggie.

"Huhman County Sheriff's —"

"It's Francis," he interrupted. "Could you round up any files we've got on Ansel Creighorn?"

"Including this most recent arrest?"

"Yes. Thanks. I'll be in soon."

Hood entered the department and beelined to the dispatch station. "Maggie," he said, "There's a connection between Travis Haulenbach and Ansel Creighorn. I don't know what it means yet, but it might be something."

"Everything we've got on Ansel is on your desk."

"Thanks."

As Hood marched to his office, Maggie called, "Oh, and Loeffelman wants you to call him as soon as possible."

Hood sat at his desk and picked up Creighorn's file. In doing so, he uncovered a stack of documents, topped by the arrest report for David Grimm. He scanned the report. The narrative from Lester Stackhouse, the responding deputy, largely corroborated Cheryl's account. He recalled their visit and her plea: *"Couldn't you just let it go?"*

Could he? Probably. But could he justify that decision?

What had Cheryl called him? Straight-laced.

Well, he reminded himself, he was straight-laced.

He also was losing his focus.

He exchanged the report for Creighorn's file and leafed through the contents, searching for the jail booking form. He located it and scanned the biographical data: Creighorn's date of birth, Nov. 14, 1978: parents' names, Dennis and Evelyn Creighorn; and place of birth, Baltimore, Maryland; education, Annapolis High School.

He retrieved Travis Haulenbach's biographical data sheet and scanned to date of birth, April 11, 1979, and education, Annapolis High School.

Hood was excited. The connection provided traction, a path to follow. Had the two men known each other during their time together in Maryland? If so, what was their relationship? Did Haulenbach travel to Huhman County to reconnect with Creighorn? If so, for what reason? Would that reason implicate Creighorn in Haulenbach's death and exonerate Herman? Hood was eager to share his discovery with someone. He was partially out of his chair when he checked himself. The link was tenuous, at best. It hardly cracked open the case, but it deserved to be investigated.

He dropped back in his chair. Although his body was still, his mind fixated on Cheryl's question, *"Couldn't you just let it go?"* He knew he couldn't. Why was he obsessing over something that had been resolved? Hood was reminded of his experience in early sobriety, when he continued to obsess over the desire to take a drink after he had resolved not to. Why, he wondered, did Cheryl's plea continue to haunt him?

He called the medical examiner.

"Loeffelman," the familiar voice answered.

"It's your sheriff," Hood said.

"I finished my final report on Haulenbach," Loeffelman said. "Nothing new. I'm ready to release the body to ship to — where'd you say?"

"Maryland," Hood said. "His former guardians are listed as next of kin."

"Okay. I'll have my assistant — "

"I'll go, too," Hood blurted into the receiver, surprising himself.

After a pause, Loeffelman asked. "Why?"

Hood wasn't sure. Part of him wanted to converse, face to face, with Haulenbach's guardians. Part of him felt no person's remains should be shipped home unaccompanied, like some baggage. And part of him wanted to get away for a while. But, mostly, he was curious about a possible link between Haulenbach and Creighorn — particularly a link that might clear his chief deputy's brother, Herman.

"Just put me on the flight," Hood told the medical examiner. He disconnected and, almost immediately, Maggie called.

"I've got Lieutenant Sauers on the line."

"Okay," he said without enthusiasm. "Put him through."

"Let me get right to the point," Sauers said when the transfer was made. "I need you to instruct Deputy Wallendorf to avoid any further involvement in the Haulenbach investigation."

"What do you mean 'further involvement?'" Hood's tone revealed puzzlement. "Wally and I had this conversation from the get-go."

"All I know is your deputy was seen talking with Ansel Creighorn and Neil Bowden."

"When? Where?"

"Yesterday evening at The Sportsmen's."

"I don't believe it," Hood said.

"Well, you'd better get to the bottom of it. As a courtesy to you, as his superior, I'm giving you a chance to straighten this out and let him know—in no uncertain terms—his actions could jeopardize the entire case."

Hood rubbed the knot tightening in the back of his neck. "I don't know what to say. I'll talk to him."

"And, as head of the task force, I'll expect an update on what you find out."

"Of course."

"Good. Then I won't take up any more of your time."

After Sauers ended the call, Hood replayed the conversation in his head. He was disturbed. He reminded himself not to form any conclusions until he had talked to Wally. Hood felt as if someone had taken a scattergun to his life. Family, job, circumstances, the investigation all were spiraling beyond his control. Before some new, unexpected wrinkle could crop up, he arose, grabbed his hat, and walked past Wally's vacant office to Maggie's dispatch station.

"I'm going out for a while," he told the dispatcher. "If Loeffelman's office calls with details for the flight to return Haulenbach's body to Maryland, write them down. I'll be going, too."

"Why?" she asked.

"Just write them down, all right? And tell Wally I need to see him. My office, 9 a.m., sharp."

Maggie looked up at him, her expression tinged with concern. "You okay?"

"Fine," he muttered.

"Oh," she added, "the prosecutor's office called. They're not going to pursue charges against . . ." she took a moment to consult a note she had written, "a David Grimm. Said we could turn him loose."

"They say why?"

"No." Maggie offered her boss a familiar release form. "It's all filled out. All I need is your signature."

Hood suspected Cheryl had taken her appeal to the prosecutor, insisted she would not testify against her husband, and prevailed. Instead of accepting the document, he asked, "When's his twenty hours up?" Maggie looked at the jail roster, the wall clock, and calculated the deadline. "About 9:45."

"I'll sign it when I get back." He left.

"Wally's in your office," Maggie said to Hood when he returned. She again extended the jail release form for David Grimm.

Hood looked at the wall clock; it read 9:22. "I meant to get back before now." He signed the document and returned it to her. "Has he been waiting long?"

"Since nine." She paused, then added, "Sharp."

"Not now," he scolded. He walked to his office and nodded to Wally, who retained the haggard look of a man suffering from too little sleep and too much anxiety. As he hung his hat on the rack, Hood said, "You were seen questioning Creighorn and Neil at The Sportsmen's last night." He settled into his desk chair. "Want to tell me what that was about?"

"I went to find my brother," Wally answered, without hesitation. "He hasn't answered my calls or returned my messages. I'm worried sick about him. I went to see if he was there, but he wasn't, so I asked Ansel and Neil if they'd seen him."

Hood waited a beat. "That's it?"

"That's it. Ansel and I exchanged maybe a couple sentences, which was mostly him threatening to tell you about the conversation. Neil tried to say something, but Ansel shut him up."

"For the record, Creighorn didn't tell me."

"And you probably can't say who did."

"No. Except somebody told somebody who told me." Hood leaned back in his chair. "And you probably already know what I'm going to say next about steering clear."

Wally nodded.

"Okay, consider it said." Hood glanced at the stack of paperwork in his inbox, which had grown during his absence. "By the way, I'm off to Maryland for a couple of days."

"Maryland? Why Maryland?"

"Why does everyone ask me that?" Hood asked, rhetorically. He had considered informing Wally of the link he had found, but—without evidence—didn't want to create false hopes. "Need to do a little fact-finding, is all."

"Okay," Wally said. "It's just that I don't want you to create the impression—like I did—of doing your own thing. Sauers would like nothing better than to call you out for some renegade investigation."

"It's a fine line sometimes," Hood said.

CHAPTER
17

Fleet Street was claustrophobic. Hood steered his rental car along the narrow street that bisected row houses protruding like variegated teeth from opposite sidewalks. Although the two-story houses were close enough to their neighbors to seem attached, each was unique. A colonial blue house trimmed in white yielded to a brick front with a light blue door and shutters, which in turn abutted a weather-beaten white facade streaked in black and shades of gray, with a faded pink door and rotting window frames.

Hood counted the house numbers until he located number 22, then edged the rental car close to the broken curb. He climbed from the confining interior and stretched to his full height. He had spent most of the day traveling before arriving at Baltimore-Washington International Airport, where he transferred Haulenbach's remains to the designated mortuary service and rented himself a compact car. He had stopped briefly at the Econo-Inn in Annapolis, but only to check in and wash up. He was eager to get started and learn what he could.

He glanced along the sidewalk, a crosshatch of bricks punctuated by clumps of tenacious grass and weeds, but saw no street signs that either prohibited or restricted parking.

GHOUL DUTY

Locking the car and pocketing the keys, he walked up the three stone steps and knocked on the door numbered 22. The man who opened the door looked tired and pale, but forced a smile. Hood, who was not in uniform, introduced himself and displayed his star as a courtesy.

"Ethan Harris," the man said. He extended a fleshy hand, and Hood grasped the offered handshake. "Come in," Mr. Harris said. "We've been expecting you." Hood followed the man into a darkened parlor. The room was littered with mismatched furniture—two sofas with frayed cushions, five well-worn armchairs, a trio of faded ottomans, and a half-dozen small tables representing a variety of styles. Lamps, books, magazines, knick-knacks, and glassware cluttered the tabletops and shelves, and an array of paintings and photographs adorned the walls. Hood surveyed the museum-like interior and saw the lifelong accumulation of a couple who clung to remnants of their past, refusing to discard their memories. What he didn't see among the photographs was a younger image of Travis Haulenbach.

The room was illuminated only dimly by light from two lamps. Heavy, floor-length drapes blocked the afternoon sun, with the exception of a sliver of light that invaded from between a narrow slit where the draperies met. Within the light, motes of dust alternately swirled and fell, stirred by Hood's arrival.

"Have a seat," Mr. Harris offered.

Hood chose an armchair beside an oval table displaying a colony of rabbits fashioned from ceramic, glass, and stone.

"Can I get you something to drink?"

Hood declined.

"My wife will join us in a minute," Mr. Harris said. "How was your trip?"

Hood described it as uneventful, then — to fill the void of silence that threatened to follow — added a vague reference to the comparative lack of humidity in Maryland.

Mr. Harris had remained standing. He listened politely, with obvious disinterest, then interrupted Hood to introduce his wife when she appeared from the kitchen. She wore a white apron over a dark, floral-print dress. A red and white tea towel was draped over her shoulder. Hood stood and greeted her, waiting patiently while she wiped her hands on the towel before accepting his handshake. She sat on one of the sofas, but Mr. Harris remained standing, as if uncomfortable in his own home.

A design coordinator might appraise the Harrises as a mismatched set, not unlike their surroundings. Mr. Harris was a small man, but slightly overweight. His receding hairline and heavy jowls betrayed the onset of old age, but it was the stoop in his posture and dullness in his eyes that indicated he had resigned himself to a future without interest or excitement. Mrs. Harris, in contrast, was obese and her demeanor severe. She wore the stern look of an angry teacher among disobedient children and appeared poised to scold at any moment.

"Ever been to Maryland before?" Mr. Harris asked,

apparently reluctant to dispense with the small talk and move on to the topic of Hood's visit.

"First time," Hood said.

"What do you think of it?" Mr. Harris asked.

"Pretty state," Hood answered, a half-truth. The fraction of Maryland he had seen during his drive from the airport had been an introduction to a day of contrasts. One moment he was enjoying an open road through forested tracts. Next, he found himself snarled in traffic congestion, amid shopping malls, restaurants, and office complexes. And now he was in a residence in a historic downtown located a few blocks from the U.S. Naval Academy and the Chesapeake Bay.

"We like it," Mr. Harris said. "How long will you be staying?"

Hood glanced at Mrs. Harris, who had remained silent. "Not long. I leave tomorrow evening." An awkward silence began to gather, prompting Hood to add, "The funeral home you selected met me at the airport. The transfer went fine."

"Good," Mr. Harris answered.

"Good?" Mrs. Harris spat the word, her entry into the conversation both brusque and unexpected. "What's good about it? Or about Travis, for that matter?"

Hood remained silent. He knew Mrs. Harris, Travis's aunt, was the elder sister of Travis's mother, who was killed outside a bar when her son was eight years old. Her ex-lover was serving a prison sentence for the crime, but he was not Travis's father. No one claimed to know the identity of Travis's father. If his mother had known, she took the information to the grave.

"He wasn't a bad boy," Mr. Harris whispered to no one in particular. Hood sensed the man was trying to convince himself, rather than his wife or his guest.

"Huh?" Mrs. Harris snapped.

"He wasn't such a bad boy, really," Mr. Harris repeated, slightly louder.

"He was," Mrs. Harris contradicted, defiantly. "I always said if he didn't mend his ways, he'd end up in jail or the graveyard. And I was right, wasn't I? First one, now the other."

Mr. Harris looked to Hood for support. "When was the last time you saw Travis?" Hood asked. He pulled a pen and small notebook from his shirt pocket and prepared to write.

"He was seventeen when he ran off for good," Mrs. Harris answered. "Why I ever took that boy in, I'll never know. I knew he was trouble." She focused on the tabletop collection of inanimate rabbits. "But she was my sister. What else could I do?" she added, not expecting a reply.

"Did he get into much trouble while he lived with you?" Hood asked.

"All the time," Mrs. Harris said. "He was wild—a wild kid." She picked at some indiscernible something on her apron. "There's nothing you can do with a wild kid, especially when he's not your own."

Hood glanced at Mr. Harris, who hadn't moved, but seemed to have receded into the clutter of the parlor.

"Was he ever taken into custody by juvenile authorities?" Hood asked.

"Oh, gracious," Mrs. Harris replied. "I don't know how many times we were called down to juvenile hall."

"Five," Mr. Harris said, a docile whisper.

"Seems like more than that," Mrs. Harris said.

"It was five," Mr. Harris said, his tone unchanged.

"Seemed like all the time to me," Mrs. Harris continued. "The last couple times, the judge made him stay at the juvenile center for a while. That's how wild he was."

"What were his offenses?" Hood asked.

She seemed momentarily puzzled by the question.

"What did he do that got him into trouble?"

"Do we really have to go into all this?" Mr. Harris asked.

"Huh?" Mrs. Harris said. She glared at her husband, apparently irritated by his contribution.

Hood suspected her repeated "huhs" were not caused by a hearing impairment; instead, they seemed habitual challenges to whatever her husband said. The sheriff looked sympathetically at Mr. Harris and said, "It might help us."

"How?" Mr. Harris said. "What's done is done."

"Huh?" Mrs. Harris said.

"I understand," Hood said, "but our job is to find out why it was done and who did it."

"I don't see how it helps to dredge up the past," Mr. Harris replied, gathering conviction.

"Let the man do his job," Mrs. Harris said. A petulant scowl clouded her expression, perhaps a reaction to being momentarily excluded from the conversation. "The sheriff came halfway across the country to talk to us and you act like the boy was some kind of angel." She turned her attention back to Hood. "He wasn't an angel," she said, loudly. "He was a liar and thief and—" she groped unsuccessfully for a word, "and he was just no good."

"You mentioned a judge earlier," Hood said. "Do you remember his name?"

"Farrington," Mr. Harris answered.

"Huh?" Mrs. Harris said.

"Farrington," Mr. Harris repeated. "He's retired now."

"That's right," his wife agreed. "Judge Farrington."

"Isn't this all available in the records?" Mr. Harris asked Hood.

Hood hesitated, unsure how to answer. Although he had reviewed Travis's background, his purpose was to probe additional links during his brief visit. "Of course," he replied, "but in my experience, I gain insights visiting with people as much as from the official record." His reply seemed to satisfy Mr. Harris, so Hood continued: "I'm assuming Travis was assigned to a juvenile officer? Do you remember his name?"

"It wasn't a him," Mrs. Harris replied. "It was a woman. Joan something, I think." She looked to her husband for clarification.

He shook his head, either unable or unwilling to help.

"Does the name Ansel Creighorn ring a bell with either of you?" Hood asked.

"That boy," Mrs. Harris said. "Talk about trouble."

"He was an older boy, a big kid," Mr. Harris added. "We think he got Travis to participate in his hijinks because—"

"Hijinks!" Mrs. Harris interrupted. "They stole a car."

"Travis said it was Ansel's idea," Mr. Harris said, "but Travis said he took the blame because he was still a juvenile and Ansel had turned eighteen and—"

"And got off scot-free is what he did," Mrs. Harris said, "while Travis spent, like, thirty days in juvenile hall."

"Do either of you know if Creighorn was ever charged with a crime?" Hood asked.

"I don't remember," Mr. Harris said. "What does it say in his record?"

Hood shook his head. In contrast to Haulenbach's juvenile record, Creighorn had no juvenile or adult criminal record in Maryland. The sheriff stood and handed Mr. Harris a business card. "If you think of anything I should know, please call," he said. He closed his notebook and replaced it and the pen in his pocket. "Thank you. I know these questions can be difficult."

"Difficult," Mrs. Harris huffed as she pushed herself, with some effort, up from the sofa. "This hasn't been difficult. Now, Travis, he was difficult."

"I'll see you out," Mr. Harris offered. He wore a defeated expression, but remained gracious, as if he had grown accustomed to the role.

Outside, Hood squinted against the bright sunlight and sneezed vigorously, as if expelling the dust he had inhaled.

He looked at Mr. Harris, who seemed even more wizened and frail in the harsh daylight.

"Thanks again," Hood said. He extended his hand and sensed from the extended handshake that Mr. Harris wanted to say something more, but was uncertain how to begin. He lingered on the step.

"My wife—" Mr. Harris began, then stopped. "We never had children of our own. We tried, but . . ." he stopped again and looked at the sheriff. "You have children?"

"A daughter," Hood answered. "Elizabeth."

"How old?"

"Fifteen." In the ensuing silence, Hood thought about his own parental anxieties. "It's never easy, raising kids, I mean. Even when you've got them from the time they're born."

Mr. Harris stared at him, and the old man's expression revealed his gratitude that Hood understood something of his shattered hopes. "I'd better get back inside," he said.

Hood nodded, but said nothing. He watched the man disappear into the darkness beyond the door and heard the lock snap into place. He walked to his rental car and started the engine. The thought of a drink wiggled into his mind. He was alone, he was a thousand miles from home, and no one would know.

Not true, he reminded himself. He would know.

CHAPTER

18

Hood slowed the rental car and peered through the dense foliage on the left, but saw no signs of the Severn River, Saltworks Creek, or the sailboat that now served as Judge Farrington's home. He pulled to the side of the road, looked again at the map the Anne Arundel County clerk had given him, and got out. He walked along the macadam road winding through the wooded area, found an unmarked path, and followed it. The thick vegetation created a dark canopy, then opened at a promontory at the top of a steep, wooden staircase. A late-morning breeze cooled his skin and rustled tree limbs, as he paused to survey the majestic panorama. Below was the narrow arm of Saltworks Creek and, gently swaying in its mooring, a double-masted sailboat that looked like a throwback to an earlier era. Beyond was the brackish Severn River, its wide expanse stretching to join the Chesapeake Bay.

A bird of prey—he wasn't sure what kind—glided in a circular path high above the water as he started down the steps, counting each as he descended. When he reached the forties, he heard the strains of a blues riff blown on a harmonica and knew he was in the right place.

The court clerk had informed him that retired Judge Caspar Farrington could be found on his boat—named "Thirty to Life"—where he either would be sailing, concocting an inventive seafood dish, or playing the blues on his guitar or harmonica. The clerk also had confirmed that Farrington's tenure as a juvenile court judge had overlapped Haulenbach's involvement in the juvenile system. According to the records, however, the juvenile officer responsible for both Haulenbach and Creighorn was Joan Flemming, who since had died of cancer.

The blues melody continued to emanate from the sailboat's cabin as Hood counted stair number sixty-eight and stepped onto the dock. He waited until the sustained notes were carried away on the breeze, then cupped his hands in front of his mouth and called, "Judge Farrington." No answer. Hood watched a jellyfish pulsate itself patiently through the water. He was preparing to call out again when a voice from the cabin bellowed, "Hang on, hang on."

The man who emerged from the belly of the boat looked like some abstract artist's work—a study in white, metallics, and muted reds, yellows, and greens. His tousled white hair and a short white beard framed a sun-bronzed face mapped with wrinkles. Sinewy, equally bronzed arms extended from an oversized shirt printed in primary colors. His muscular legs, with white hair on golden skin, extended from a pair of shorts splashed with white and yellow geometric shapes against a faded red background. A pair of worn deck shoes covered his feet, and in his right hand he held a battered harmonica. Wordlessly, he studied his visitor.

"My name's Francis Hood," the sheriff said. "I'm a county sheriff from Missouri."

The man made no reply.

Hood was about to elaborate when Farrington barked: "Lawman, huh? Got a badge?"

Hood displayed his star.

Farrington inspected it. "Never seen one like this before. Wouldn't know whether it was real or fake." He paused. "Well, come aboard then."

"Thanks, Judge Farrington."

"I'm retired," Farrington said, as he extended his hand to help Hood aboard, then pumped Hood's hand in an exuberant shake. "Enough with the judge shit. Call me Cap."

"Is that short for Caspar or captain?"

"Ha," the man laughed. "Never was a captain. I was a lieutenant, though. U.S. Navy."

"Is that where you learned to sail?"

Again, he laughed. "Hell, no. I did sub duty. Spent months at a time without seeing the sun. Like being buried alive." He looked to the skies. "But you didn't track me down all the way from Missouri to hear an old man tell war stories." He produced a penetrating stare. "Let's sit down and you can tell me what's on your mind."

They moved to the stern and sat on cushioned benches facing each other from opposite sides of a large steering wheel. Hood related the circumstances surrounding the drinking debacle at the cemetery and Travis Haulenbach's death. He also summarized Herman Wallendorf's admission, but omitted naming Ansel Creighorn or Neil Bowden. He concluded by characterizing his mission as an effort to learn more about Haulenbach's past.

"Court open the records to you?" Cap asked.

"Yes."

"So why come see me?"

"I thought maybe you could tell me something more, since you were the juvenile judge then." Hood shrugged. "Maybe something that could help with the case."

Cap studied the sheriff's expression. "Spend any time on the water?"

Hood hesitated as he admired the sailboat's teak deck, its gleaming brass hardware and complex rigging that seemed to connect everything to something else. "Rivers," he answered finally, without revealing his apprehension about boating. "I've never sailed."

"Then you're in for a treat," Cap moved to the bow and began casting off lines.

"I don't know," Hood said, a gracious protest.

"Well, I'm going sailing now." Cap returned to the wheelhouse and took hold of the remaining line hitched to a dock cleat. "So we can either cast off or you can step off."

Hood liked Cap and his no-nonsense approach. He suspected if anyone knew more about a past connection between Haulenbach and Creighorn, it might be the wily old judge. And he hadn't come this far to abandon ship prematurely. "Cast off, then," he said. Cap started the engine, and within moments they were churning toward open water.

GHOUL DUTY

The breeze freshened as they moved away from the confines of the steep embankments of sheltering Saltworks Creek. Cutting the motor, Cap began cranking two of the four chrome-plated ratchets at the helm. Hood watched as first the main sail, then a smaller, triangular one, unfurled and harnessed the wind.

Hood felt his anxiety yield to exhilaration as the powerful sailboat sliced through the choppy water.

"What kind of boat is this?" he asked.

"Cutter ketch," Cap answered, as he adjusted lines and sails. "Forty-seven feet from bowsprit to stern."

"It's quite a boat," Hood said, his praise sincere.

"That she is," Cap agreed.

The sailboat, despite its size, apparently was designed so it could be handled by a solitary seaman, and Hood was mesmerized by Cap's singular concentration as he trimmed the sails to satisfaction. The man's movements, like his words, were sparse and efficient. Hood sensed Caspar Farrington had been an excellent judge; he was an intent listener, a penetrating inquisitor, and a commanding presence. Cap finished his adjustments and relaxed behind the wheel as he guided them along their course.

"How'd you come up with the name for her?" Hood asked, adopting the feminine pronoun.

"Thirty to Life? My wife used to say that's how long it would take to pay it off." He focused on the horizon. "She's gone now — died a little over three years ago. When I retired,

I decided to sell the house and move to the boat. Now, I figure thirty to life is how long I'm gonna live here."

Hood smiled. "How long have you been retired?"

"Nearly two years. Hit the mandatory retirement age of seventy. Now I sail, play some music, do some fishing." He faced Hood. "What kind of fishing trip you on, Sheriff?"

"Well, I told you about the drunk-fest at the cemetery and how one guy, Herman, admitted whacking Haulenbach with a shovel, but not necessarily killing him. What I didn't tell you is Herman is the brother of my chief deputy. My deputy's pretty stoic, but I can tell it's tearing him up, thinking his kid brother may have killed somebody."

Cap rubbed his beard, as if anticipating Hood hadn't finished.

"I also found out," the sheriff continued, "one of the other guys at the cemetery knew Travis when they were younger and both lived in Maryland. Name's Ansel Creighorn. By the way, I looked for Creighorn's name in the court records, but came up empty."

"Ansel Creighorn," Cap repeated, his tone revealing recognition.

"You remember him."

"I always seem to remember odd names."

"Haulenbach's guardians seem to think Creighorn, who was older, used Haulenbach to take the fall because he was still a juvenile."

"Sounds right. I knew Creighorn by name and reputation, but I don't remember him ever coming before my court. If memory serves, the kid didn't reform or change his ways. His family just left town and moved west."

"Do you know of any reason Haulenbach might have tracked him down in Missouri, maybe to settle some score or blackmail him for something?"

Cap shrugged. "Can't help you."

Hood frowned.

"You want a beer?" Cap asked, signaling the topic of conversation was closed.

"I shouldn't," Hood said.

"Suit yourself." Cap arose from his seat. "Hold the wheel," he instructed. "Keep us pointed at the tower up ahead while I raid the fridge." He headed for the cabin and, as he descended from view, asked, "You sure you don't want one?"

"I better not," Hood said.

Hood swayed unsteadily as he walked, a result—ironically—of sailing, not drinking. In no hurry to leave for the airport, he checked out of the hotel, loaded his bags in the rental car, and crossed the parking lot to an adjacent restaurant, where the meal he was served last night had been excellent. He sat at a small table and studied the menu. Last night he had enjoyed a cup of Maryland crab soup and blackened grouper. He was trying to decide between some type of steak or seafood when his ringtone indicated an incoming text message. The display showed it was from

Sandra Brondel, the crime lab technician and task force member. The message was: "Call me."

He did.

After an obligatory exchange of greetings and weather comparisons, she said, "I've got some results from the Haulenbach case. I forwarded a report to the others, but I wasn't sure if you were checking email, so I thought I'd give you a call."

"Thanks. What's up?"

"Well, first, Haulenbach's apartment was immaculate. The landlord should give the cleaning crew a raise. We found some prints where people usually don't wipe down—doorknobs, the fridge handle—but the ones that aren't smudged all belong to Haulenbach."

"Figures," Hood said, slightly exasperated.

"But evidence from the trucks and tools told a different story," Sandra continued. "Nothing links Herman to Haulenbach's death, but," she paused, "are you ready for this?"

He wasn't sure how to respond. "Okay," he ventured.

"A shovel in Ansel Creighorn's pickup had traces of Haulenbach's blood and tissue on the back of the blade. And the only prints on the handle are Creighorn's."

Hood hesitated before responding. "Sounds pretty incriminating," he said. "Has anyone talked to Creighorn yet?"

"Don't know, but I don't think so. I just sent out the report."

Hood wished he was home so he could summon the task force to discuss the findings and plan their next move.

"I'll be back tonight," he said, "but not until about ten. I don't arrive in St. Louis until after seven."

"I don't think anything will happen until tomorrow. Want me to keep you posted if there are any new developments?"

"Please."

After they disconnected, a waitress approached and recited the specials. Hood opted for crab-stuffed flounder with wild rice and seasoned vegetables. He was content to drink water, sipped as he contemplated Sandra's information. The blood and tissue indicated the shovel found in Creighorn's truck had been used to strike—but not necessarily kill—Haulenbach. And although the fingerprints implicated Creighorn, the evidence didn't prove he'd struck the blow. Hood made a mental note to ask Sandra if a pair or pairs of work gloves were in the trucks. He reviewed what he had learned about the connection between Haulenbach and Creighorn, and decided it offered no new evidence or direction. When his meal was served, he reminded himself to eat unhurriedly. He was eager to move, but, for the present, he had no place to go.

Hood anticipated another solitary evening following a long day that began in Maryland, included a flight halfway across the country, and ended with a two-hour drive from St. Louis. He was mentally and physically exhausted when he turned into his neighborhood, anticipating what he hoped would be a night of sound sleep. As he steered into his driveway, he immediately recognized the woman who sat on the top step of his front porch. She was stooped over, with her head bent forward and waves of her long blonde hair obscuring her face.

Hood was dumbfounded. He got out of his vehicle, approached, and pronounced her name as a whispered question—"Cheryl?" She looked up, revealing a lost expression, with reddened eyes and cheeks wet with tears. As Hood stepped forward, Cheryl stood and wrapped her arms around him and rested her head on his shoulder.

Hood didn't pull away immediately; he held her consolingly. When he felt the embrace had lasted too long, he loosened his hold and was relieved when she released him and stepped back.

"I left him," she said.

"Did he hurt you again?"

"He didn't hit me again, if that's what you mean, but it hurts every time he gets drunxk."

"I understand," Hood said. He didn't entirely. He knew what it was like to be alcoholic. He had no experience being the spouse of someone who was chronically intoxicated.

"I don't know him anymore," Cheryl said. "He's not the man I married."

Hood thought of his wife, Linda, who said she had to leave because she couldn't endure the trauma of watching helplessly as he committed slow-motion suicide. "You can get an order of protection from—"

"No, no, no." Her staccato response shot down the

suggestion. "That would just piss him off more than ever. I never thought I'd say this, but he frightens me. I'm already worried he'll come after me."

"Where's your car?"

"My car has my name and face splashed on the side," she said, reminding Hood she was a real estate agent. "I called a cab. I'm not driving around in a car that shouts 'Here I am.'"

"So?" Hood said, slurring the syllable into an open-ended question.

"So, what am I going to do?"

"Yes."

"I don't know. It was a spur-of-the-moment thing. I didn't even pack a bag."

"Surely, you have relatives, friends who can take you in."

"There's a girlfriend I could call. She might be willing to put me up for a night or two."

Hood's thoughts were awash in confusion. He realized, almost simultaneously, that Cheryl had not formulated a plan, and that her spontaneous decision had brought her to his door. What did she expect him to do? Did she expect him, somehow, to solve her dilemma? The question he asked was, "How did you even find me?"

"I'm in real estate. I know where people live. I've used your name three or four times with prospective buyers in this neighborhood. You wouldn't believe how many people feel safer living near a law enforcement officer." Cheryl's tone brightened as the topic turned to her sales pitch. "You've helped me close a few deals, Francis."

Her flattery was a fleeting distraction, quickly replaced by new questions. Was she aware of his separation from his wife? Did she expect him to invite her to stay? All he asked was, "What do you propose?"

"I thought maybe you'd have some ideas."

Hood shrugged. "Hotel?"

"I considered that, but then I thought David might check the hotels."

"Lock the door." Hood said, trying to hide any hint of the confusion he was experiencing. "Call security if he finds you."

"I'd rather not be alone right now." When Hood said nothing, she added, "I heard your wife and daughter had moved out."

"Cheryl, this is not—" Hood began. He let the remainder of the sentence vanish in the evening stillness as they awkwardly faced each other.

Finally, Cheryl said, "I guess I'd better call my girlfriend."

"I think that's best."

CHAPTER
19

Hood arrived early for the late-morning session.

Creighorn had agreed to meet with task force members in the interview room at the police station. Hood was eager to hear the big man's explanation about why his truck contained the apparent murder weapon, a shovel with his fingerprints on the handle and Travis Haulenbach's blood and tissue on the blade. He also wanted to gauge Creighorn's reaction to what Hood had learned during his trip to Maryland.

The sheriff was directed to Sauers' office, where the police lieutenant was conferring with the other members of the investigation team—Sandra Brondel from the crime lab and the patrol's Tim Johnson. They exchanged greetings and Sauers began briefing Hood. "As I understand it, Sandra has already told you the only evidence was found on a shovel in Creighorn's pickup. Obviously, we kept the shovel, but released the vehicles and other tools to their owners. Tim and Sandra also interviewed Neil Bowden again this morning. All they got from Neil was a repeat of his see-no-evil, hear-no-evil, I-was-asleep-in-the-truck speech."

Hood, in turn, reported Creighorn and Haulenbach were involved in criminal activity while Creighorn was a young adult and Haulenbach was a juvenile. He described the crimes and the disparity in culpability and punishment separating the duo.

"Let's work that into the questioning," Sauers said. "For the sake of consistency, I thought Francis and I should re-interview Creighorn. Tim and Sandra will monitor from behind the glass. I'll ask him to repeat his account of what happened at the cemetery, then have Francis inquire about Creighorn's relationship with the victim, and I'll finish up by informing him about the evidence found on the shovel. I think we need to go slow on this. Those prints on the shovel are pretty incriminating, but won't hold up as proof."

"I'm thinking the same thing," Hood said. He turned to Sandra, "Were there work gloves in the trucks?"

"Both," she answered.

"So anybody could have put on gloves," Hood said.

"Exactly," Sauers agreed. "And right now the only eyewitness who says he saw or remembers anything is Creighorn, and we all—"

A knock on the door stopped Sauers in mid-sentence. He opened the door to a fellow officer, who reported Creighorn and his attorney Albert Vanderfeltz had arrived and were waiting in the interrogation room.

Once inside, Sauers began with the routine disclaimer that he and Hood wanted to hear Creighorn's narrative once more in case they had missed something. Everyone in the room knew the authorities' actual intent—to identify and inquire about any inconsistencies in Creighorn's two versions. Creighorn, however, was consistent. His retelling of events matched his initial version almost identically.

Sauers looked at Hood, who leaned forward, rested his elbows on the table, and addressed Creighorn. "You knew Travis Haulenbach before he moved here in the spring, didn't you?"

"Yeah. I knew him as a kid."

"You attended Annapolis High School at the same time, but you graduated a year before him. Is that correct?"

"Yeah. So?"

"So, were you two ever involved in criminal activity in Maryland?"

"My record's clean. You can check."

"I did," Hood said. "I also talked to sources who believe you had Haulenbach take the fall because you were an adult and he was a juvenile."

"Or maybe he was the criminal and I was just in the wrong place at the wrong time."

"Did Haulenbach look you up when he came out here this spring?"

"What do you mean 'look me up'?"

"Did he contact you before or after he came out here?"

"Not before."

"Herman Wallendorf said you introduced him to Haulenbach."

Creighorn shrugged. "I guess that's right."

"So you and Haulenbach did make contact at some point?"

"Maybe. Maybe he came by my place, maybe we just ran into each other at The Sportsmen's. I don't remember."

Hood rubbed his chin. "You're saying you were reunited with someone you knew pretty well in high school, decades ago in Maryland, and you don't remember the circumstances."

"Okay. So he looked me up. Wanted to borrow money. Wanted to know if I'd join up on some petty burglary he was planning. I told him I wasn't interested. I told him I owned my business these days. I told him if he needed money, I'd give him a job."

"Did you?"

"Did I what?"

"Give him a job."

"He didn't want it. Said he didn't want to be a ditch digger."

"But after you introduced him to Herman, Haulenbach accepted a job digging graves."

"Yeah. Go figure."

"What was your relationship with Travis Haulenbach?"

"Relationship? There was no relationship. He was a fuck-up when I knew him in Maryland, and he was a fuck-up out here. Guys like that don't change."

"But you hung out with him."

"More like he hung out with me, but mostly when Herman was around."

Hood felt he had exhausted his line of inquiry. In the silence that followed, Sauers retrieved his lead role. "Going back to that night at the cemetery," he said, "You claimed Herman hit Haulenbach with a shovel. Which truck did Herman get the shovel from—his or yours?"

"His, I guess," Creighorn said. "Wasn't really watching." He slumped in his chair, his posture signaling disinterest.

"Did you notice whose shovel it was?" Sauers continued.

"Nope."

"Could you identify it if you saw it?"

"If it's mine, probably." Creighorn glanced at his attorney. "What's all this about a shovel?"

"We'll get to that. Was Herman wearing gloves?"

"Gloves? It was spring."

"Work gloves."

"We were drinking. Why would he be wearing work gloves?"

"What would you say if I told you we found samples of Haulenbach's blood and tissue on the back of one of the shovel blades?"

Creighorn sat up slightly, his attention piqued. "I'd say that proved what I told you. That's the shovel Herman used."

"And what if I told you the shovel was in your truck and the only fingerprints on it—specifically, on the handle—are yours?"

"What the fuck are you trying—" Ansel began before being halted by his attorney.

"Are these 'what if' questions based on conjecture or fact?" Vanderfeltz asked.

"Oh, they're facts, all right," Sauers said.

"Do you intend to charge my client with a crime based on these facts?" the attorney asked, nearly sneering the word "facts."

"Not at this time."

"Then I advise my client to refuse to answer any further questions right now." He pushed back his chair and stood. "We're done here."

Lisa answered the knock at the door. "Heath," she said, her surprise apparent. He looked at her wet black hair cascading along the shoulders of the white terry cloth robe, then followed the contours of her body, hidden by the fabric but revealed in his imagination.

"Hi Lisa," he said, bringing his gaze back to her face.

"What brings you out here?"

"I was just wondering," Schrock began. He felt warmth flush his face—evidence of the wave of embarrassment rippling through him. "I was just around—around here, I mean—and I thought maybe we could get something to eat."

"I've got to work," she answered, still holding the door ajar, but physically blocking his entry.

"Yeah, well, maybe later. After work. There's that 24-hour place—"

"Heath," she said. She looked down at her bare feet. "I'm sorry if I gave you the wrong impression or anything. I liked hearing about Buddy, and you seem like an okay guy and maybe being around you made me feel closer to him somehow, but—" she lifted her head, made eye contact, and added, "I'm married."

"Yeah, well, sure. I knew that when we met." He shrugged. "I mean, that's why I looked you up. I figured I could tell you some about Buddy and, you know—"

"Stop. Okay?"

"Yeah, sure." He looked away.

"I've got to finish getting ready."

"Okay."

"Okay," she said. She closed the door between them.

Although Hood was aware Cheryl lived in an upscale neighborhood, he had underestimated the grandeur of the executive home they approached. A circular driveway led to the stone facade of the French country-style house situated on a lush, well-maintained lawn. As Wally parked the cruiser, Hood guessed the cost of the shrubbery alone exceeded his annual salary.

The trio—Hood, Wally, and Cheryl—got out and climbed the wide stone steps. "I called ahead," Cheryl said, as she extracted a key from her purse, "so David knows we're coming. He'll probably be here." She unlocked and opened one of the twin, ornate oak doors.

They entered a large foyer, where David stood on the bottom step of a sweeping circular staircase. He held a drink and swayed slightly, obviously intoxicated.

Cheryl and David stared at each other for a silent

moment before David said, "About time you stopped this nonsense and came home."

"I'm not staying," Cheryl said. "I'm just here to get some of my things."

"That why you brought them with you?" He pointed to Hood and Wally.

"Yes."

"Cheryl." David spread his hands in gesture of apology. "Look, I'm sorry. I know things have gotten a little crazy lately, but that's because I love you. You know I do. It's just— can we just talk for a few minutes, in private?"

"No." Cheryl's voice was firm. "I need some time to think. I just need—"

"At least tell me where you're staying."

"No. I need some time."

David stepped onto the floor and approached his wife, prompting Hood to close the distance and stand beside Cheryl.

"I just want to talk to my wife," David said to the sheriff.

"And she obviously doesn't want to talk to you," Hood countered.

"She came here, to my house." David's tone revealed increasing anger.

"Our house," Cheryl said.

"She came to get some personal items," Hood said. "She has a right to do that without being harassed."

"Is that what I'm doing, Cheryl? Harassing you?"

"David," Hood said. "Your wife is here to retrieve some of her belongings. I need you to let her —"

"I'm trying to talk to you," David said to his wife, ignoring the sheriff, "I just want to tell you I'm sorry. I'll make it up to you. I will."

"I'm going upstairs to pack," Cheryl replied, her tone intentionally unemotional. "I'd appreciate it if you'd stay down here."

She was in mid-step when David reached out and seized her forearm, causing her to wince. Hood reacted, grasping David's upper arm in a powerful grip. "Let her go," the sheriff warned.

"Or what?" David produced an arrogant chuff. "Now you think you're Mister Authority with your uniform, your gun, your deputy standing there. Behind all that you're still the same snot-nosed coward I beat up in high school."

Hood knew he was being baited. He knew he couldn't back down, but at the same time knew he needed to contain his rising anger.

"Remember that day?" David taunted. "Remember how I rubbed your bloody nose into the dirt in front of everybody?" David turned to his wife. "Remember that, Cheryl?"

"Let her go," Hood commanded.

David released her arm. Hood was surprised and relieved the confrontation hadn't escalated. Cheryl began climbing the staircase.

"So this is your hero, now?" David called to her. He faced Hood, raised his glass, and downed its contents, letting the ice clink against his teeth. "She's all yours," he said. "I don't need this shit." He walked into the kitchen, leaving Hood and Wally standing in the foyer.

"Wait here," Hood said to his deputy, then followed David, who was refilling his tumbler with ice from the refrigerator door dispenser. The sheriff watched the man remove the cap from a vodka bottle on the counter and fill the tumbler to the brim.

"What are you looking at?" David asked.

Hood wanted to say what he felt—that he was looking at his reflection. Instead, he said, "There's a solution, David. I know people who have found it."

David sneered. "What're you talking about?"

"I'm talking about alcohol. I was, I am—" Hood stopped himself in mid-sentence. He wasn't ready to share his own experience. He needed time to ponder the potential consequences.

"Look," David said, "I don't need anything from you. Just get the fuck out of my house."

Hood removed a business card and pen from his pocket. He leaned over the kitchen's center island and wrote New Opportunities, Huhman County Hospital, on the back of the card. "This is for you," Hood said, "in case you ever want it."

Lisa drove her battered Ford from the parking lot of her apartment complex on her way to drop off Cody. She switched her wiper blades from intermittent to fast in a futile attempt to keep pace with the sheets of rain cascading down her windshield. Even within the confines of her car and amid the downpour, she heard the sharp honks of a horn, causing her to wonder what was wrong—was a brake light out, had she inadvertently cut off the driver behind her, was a tire going flat?

She glanced at her son in the passenger seat. Cody was belted securely. As she looked at the indicator lights on the dashboard, she sensed movement outside her vehicle. Adrenaline coursed through her as she watched the blurred shape of a white pickup attempting to pass. The truck sped ahead and cut in front of her, forcing her to trounce on the brakes and veer sharply. The front passenger side of her car jumped the curb, and the tire sank into the sodden strip of grass separating street from sidewalk. In the instant her car stopped, Lisa flung open the door. "Stay here, Cody." She stepped into the raindrops and met the driver of the Creighorn Excavating Co. pickup.

"Are you crazy, Ansel?" she shouted at the giant, who no longer was encumbered by a sling. "I've got my son in the car. What the hell are you—"

A hard slap on her cheek stopped her in mid-sentence. She pressed her palm to her face, more stunned than injured.

"Where can I find that punk?" Creighorn spat.

Lisa nearly laughed at the strand of spittle hanging from his lower lip. "Who're you talking about?"

"Your boyfriend. Bobby Schrock's kid."

"First, he's not my boyfriend. He's—"

"So why's he always hangin' around you like some lovesick—"

"He doesn't know anybody. He just got out of the joint. He knows Buddy from—"

"I don't care who he knows or what he knows. What I want to know is where to find him."

Lisa shook her head. "I have no idea."

"You putting him up at your place?"

"No," she shouted, her indignation apparent.

When Creighorn moved to hit her again, she lunged at him, tying him up in a mass of flailing arms. They staggered as one along the sidewalk, careened into a large plastic trash container, and toppled over. Cody leaped from the car and jumped on Creighorn. "Leave my mom alone," the boy screamed as he pummeled Creighorn on the back. Creighorn scrambled to his knees, the boy still clinging to his back. He flung Cody to the ground in the same instant he kicked Lisa in the side.

He looked alternately at Cody and Lisa. Neither appeared eager to resume the struggle. "When you see Schrock," he told Lisa, "you tell him I'm gonna find him. You tell him he's dead meat."

Hood awoke to a persistent, annoying sound, momentarily uncertain of its origin. He propped himself on his elbow and turned to the nightstand while his semi-consciousness recognized the ringing of his cell phone.

"This is your sheriff," he answered with the little enthusiasm he was able to muster. He glanced at the digital clock, which read 2:12 a.m.

Hearing no response except a faint ticking, he sat up in bed and held the phone more closely to his ear. The sound of a clock was distinct.

"Hello," he said.

No response. The ticking continued.

"Schrock," he said, loudly. "If it's you, talk to me."

Tick, tick, tick, tick . . .

"Talk to me or I'm hanging up."

Tick, tick, tick, tick . . .

Hood pressed disconnect and immediately called his wife.

After several rings, she answered. "Hello." Her voice sounded groggy.

"Linda, it's me, Francis."

"Francis? What time is it?"

"After two. I just got a bizarre phone call and I wanted to check and make sure you're okay."

"I'm fine. What phone call?"

"Don't know. No one spoke."

"Wrong number?"

"Probably," Hood said. He was hoping to ease her mind. "Would you do me a favor? Would you check on Elizabeth for me."

"She's not here. She's spending the night with Claire."

"Spending the night?" Hood attempted to mask any alarm in his tone.

"Yes, with Claire. What's going on, Francis?"

"It's fine. Do you have their phone number?" he asked, realizing that although he knew the address from dropping off or picking up his daughter, he didn't have any contact number. "I want to call over there and —"

"You're scaring me, Francis. What's going on that you're not telling me?"

"Nothing. I'm sure it's nothing. I'm probably just overreacting. Do me a favor, call the Reinkemeyer's number and tell them I'm going to come by. And ask them to lock their doors, and not open them to anyone but me."

"If you're going over there, I'm going, too," Linda said.

Hood knew better than to argue.

The early-morning reunion of the Hood family at the Reinkemeyer household quickly disintegrated from relief to confusion. After hugging his daughter and reassuring the families that everything was fine, Hood felt the need to say something about his actions. He didn't know where to begin or how much to say. Not helping was the presence of the Reinkemeyers, who seemed uncertain of their role or what to do next.

"I'm sorry," Hood began. "I probably overreacted, but things have been a little crazy lately." He glanced at Warren Reinkemeyer, then at Warren's wife and daughter. He knew them, but not well. He couldn't recall much about previous conversations with them. He turned back to his wife. "Maybe we should talk about this," he paused and lowered his voice to a whisper, "just you and me."

The shared expressions among the Reinkemeyers indicated they got the hint. "We'll get some coffee started," Mrs. Reinkemeyer said. She left for the kitchen, dutifully followed by her husband and daughter.

"You go, too," Linda instructed Elizabeth. When their daughter also adjourned to the kitchen, Linda said, "You need to tell me what's going on."

"I honestly don't know. My cell rang right before I called you, and the only sound was a ticking clock. The only connection I can think of is the words Heath Schrock said to me after —"

"I remember," Linda said, "but what's that got to do with Elizabeth? You don't think she's in danger, do you?"

"I don't know."

She was silent for a long time. "I'm frightened," she said, finally.

Hood embraced her. He was frightened, too. And angry. He wanted — no, needed — to do something, but had no idea what action to take. He held her tightly, but said nothing.

CHAPTER
20

The swing set dominating the apartment playground was a triangular structure of peeling paint and rusted metal. Two of three swings were functional; the other dangled from a single chain. The dried mud below was sculpted by repeated shoe scuffs and bordered by clumps of weeds. Lisa's son, Cody, sat on one of the usable swings, swaying slightly and watching his sneakers trace the parallel ruts. As Heath Schrock approached, the boy looked up, revealing an angry red scrape from forehead to cheek.

"Wow," Schrock said, eyeing the bruise. He leaned his weight against the swing set's A-frame. "How'd you get that?"

Cody focused again on his sneakers. "I'm not supposed to say."

"According to who?"

"My mom."

"You get in a fight?"

Cody shook his head. "I can take anybody my size."

"Big kid?"

"Wasn't no kid."

"A grown-up?"

"Big guy," Cody answered.

Schrock hesitated. "This guy happen to have bushy black hair and a big black beard?"

Cody looked up. "If I say any more, I might get in trouble," he said, both an explanation and an apology.

An awkward silence followed before Schrock asked, "Your mom home?"

Cody gestured with his thumb toward the apartment complex. As Schrock turned to walk away, Cody said, "Do me a favor?"

Schrock looked back at the boy. "Name it."

"Don't tell my mom about how bad she looks."

Schrock left Cody on the swing, climbed the stairs to Lisa's apartment, and hammered on the door.

No answer.

He hammered some more.

Again, no answer.

"Lisa," he shouted. "I know you're in there. I saw Cody outside."

"I can't see you now," she called from inside the door. "Come back another time."

"No good, Lisa. Let me in."

"I don't think it's a good idea."

"Look," Schrock said. "I talked to Cody, and I'm pretty sure I know who did this—and he's gonna pay, whether you open the door or not."

He heard the lock click and watched the door open. He wasn't prepared for the sight of Lisa's face. Her left cheekbone appeared swollen and bruised, leaving her eye partially closed.

Her upper lip was stitched where it had been split on the left side, and at least one tooth was noticeably chipped.

"God damn him," Schrock said, visibly seething. He brushed past her and paced the living room. "God damn him to hell. God damn coward, beating on a woman and a kid. When I'm done with him, he'll know what hell is because—"

"No," Lisa interrupted, grabbing his arms. He stopped pacing, looked at her and winced. "You'll just end up back in prison."

"I don't really give a—"

"I do," she said. "Ansel Creighorn's not worth it. He's baiting you. I'm sure of it."

Her words seemed to have a calming effect because Schrock stepped forward and enfolded her in his arms. "Don't worry," he said, his tone soothing. "It's gonna be fine." He stroked her long hair with his fingers and pulled her face nearer, feeling her warm breath on his neck in the instant before she tried to pull back. He held her tightly, but her tension and resistance were unmistakable. When he relaxed his grip, she separated herself and stepped away. "This is wrong," she said.

"What?" he asked, acting surprised. "I wasn't tryin' to—" he began. "Did you think—?"

She held up her hand. "I'm—I'm a mess right now," she said. "I'm not thinking straight."

Schrock looked at her for a long moment. "Maybe, I should just go."

Lisa nodded.

GHOUL DUTY

*****

The ringing phone awakened a napping Dwayne Rehagen, a Missouri Department of Corrections officer who supplemented his modest state salary by ferrying information – among other things – inside and outside the prison walls.

"Yeah," he answered.

"It's Heath Schrock."

"Heath. How's life on the outside?"

"So far, so good. Need to get a message to Jimmy."

The two men negotiated arranging an exchange between Heath and Jimmy Kronk, as well as a fee for Rehagen's services.

The Schrock cousins sat on the tailgate of Ronnie's truck, chewing the pre-packaged sandwiches and sipping the beers they had bought at a convenience store. They ate wordlessly, cooled by their drying perspiration from the exertion of mowing three lawns during the sultry, humid morning.

"I'm thinking we should get our own place," Ronnie said, breaking their silence.

"I thought you liked living with Freddie," Heath replied. "What'd you call it – a 'sweet deal'?" He studied his cousin, then asked, "Or was this Freddie's idea?"

"No. Nothing like that," Ronnie said, a half-truth. Although Freddie knew better than to threaten, he had suggested strongly to Ronnie that his cousin begin contributing to rent and expenses, or clear out, preferably the latter. "It's just—I mean, you're sleeping on that crappy sofa in the living room."

"Beats a prison mattress."

Ronnie shrugged. "It's whatever, you know. Truth is, I'm worried sooner or later Freddie's gonna get busted with all that dope, and if you're living there, they'll yank your parole and toss you back inside."

"Look at you looking out for me," Heath quipped.

"We're blood."

"We are," Heath affirmed. "Okay, I'm sick of Freddie's shit, anyway. Let's find us a place."

"Okay," Ronnie said.

The cousins sat wordlessly, alternately chewing and sipping, until Ronnie asked, "So, what's with you and the sheriff? You done with all that?"

Heath shrugged. "I've got another trick up my sleeve, but—to tell you the truth—I've got other priorities now."

"Like that girl you been tracking on?"

"Leave it," Heath said. His tone was light, but an unmistakable warning was implied.

"All I'm saying is if some tease was—" Ronnie began, stopping abruptly when Heath grabbed his hand and jammed the remainder of his sandwich into his teeth.

Heath released his grip and stared intently at Ronnie.

"Are you crazy?" Ronnie shouted, spitting fragments of meat and bread and wiping mustard from his lips.

"'Leave it means leave it the fuck alone. I shouldn't have

to tell you twice. Understood?" He waited until Ronnie acknowledged the admonition with a nod.

Hood informed Maggie he would be late, but didn't give a reason. He had spent the morning arranging security for his wife and daughter, including enlisting two retired deputies to watch them. When he entered the department and greeted Maggie, he saw—in the periphery of his vision—someone seated in one of the visitors' chairs adjacent to the dispatch station.

"A Cheryl Grimm is waiting to see you," Maggie told her boss while, as if on cue, Cheryl stood and approached.

Hood swiveled his head from Cheryl, to Maggie, and back to Cheryl.

"Can I talk to you?" Cheryl asked him.

Hood nodded.

"In private?" she added.

"Sure." As he spoke, he caught a glimpse of Maggie's cautionary expression. Hood was aware of Maggie's innate ability to assess human behaviors, which she would share only if asked. In the moment before he turned to escort Cheryl to his office, he gave Maggie a nod of understanding.

"How long have you been waiting?" Hood asked Cheryl as they entered his office. Closing the door, he waited until she settled into one of the visitors' chairs, then sat behind his desk.

"About an hour."

"An hour," he repeated. "So, what can I do for you?"

"I've been thinking, Francis. Actually, I find myself doing that a lot lately. And, well, I don't know quite how to say this."

Hood waited. Experience had taught him silence sometimes was more effective than coaxing.

"I think," she continued, "marrying David was a mistake. I mean, I see now that our marriage is a mistake. It's a sham. It was all built on appearances. He was the star athlete. I was the perky cheerleader. We raised two successful boys, David had a great job, we have nice cars, live in a beautiful home. Now, it's all crumbling. The boys are grown and gone. David started drinking and doing drugs. He lost his job. I don't know if you know that. We're in debt, way in debt. And then," she added, choking the words, "the abuse—"

Struggling to compose herself, she pulled a tissue from her purse and held it in her lap with the fingers of both hands. "I told myself that he was hurting, that he'd lost his self-esteem and was taking it out on me." She used the tissue to dab a corner of her eye. "But I don't think so. I honestly don't think he ever loved me. He said things to me he couldn't have said if he ever loved me. I was just another one of his possessions, something he acquired to make—"

She began crying. She struggled to restrain it, but failed.

Hood was unsure how to react to the convulsive weeping that followed. He waited silently, offering no consoling words, gestures or contact. Eventually the sobbing abated. Cheryl looked at him with reddened, watery, expectant eyes, as if he would know what to do.

"Do you have someone—a priest, a counselor—you could discuss this—?"

"There's no one I trust."

"You're trusting me," Hood said. He regretted blurting the words in the moment he spoke them.

A brief silence ensued before Cheryl said, "I've always been able to trust you, Francis."

Hood was simultaneously flattered and disarmed by the comment.

"I've been thinking a lot about the choices we make," Cheryl continued. "How people's lives could have been so different if they had just made a different choice along the way."

"Well, I guess we can always wonder about the 'what ifs,' but it doesn't really change anything."

"It can. If people recognize missed opportunities, sometimes it's not too late to change, to make things right."

Hood wasn't certain where the conversation was going, but he knew he had become uncomfortable, perhaps because his life had become uncomfortable. He knew he was lonely. He blamed himself for his drinking and for splintering his family. But the only change he wanted was to put things back together.

"I've got a meeting to get to," he said, a half-truth. He stood.

"I understand," Cheryl said. "Another time, perhaps." She left.

* * * * *

"As a result of my higher power not giving up on me five minutes before the miracle happened, today I'm a grateful, recovering alcoholic, and my name is Ed."

"Hi, Ed."

Although Hood mechanically chimed in with the group's greeting at the evening meeting, he wanted to be someplace else. Where, exactly, he wasn't certain. He was unable to focus, but he feigned attentiveness as Ed droned on about the "old days" when he attended meetings in St. Louis, where the "old timers" had "a lot of sobriety." Ed spoke almost reverently about how, back then, an alcoholic had to "hit rock bottom" before he was ready to "fall on his knees" and "surrender to a higher power I choose to call God the creator." Hood was considering getting up and walking out when Ed finally ended his harangue.

When the next to speak was Mac, Hood refocused. He often found helpful suggestions in what Mac shared. The man seemed to have an uncommon ability to articulate how he used recovery principles to improve his attitude toward himself and his life. "I don't know if I ever hit rock bottom," Mac said. "I've heard people in recovery say the elevator of addiction goes all the way to Hell, but you can get off at any time. I may not have gone all the way to Hell, but I could sure see it from where I was. I was mired in shame, and I don't use that word loosely. For me, shame is different from guilt."

Hood leaned forward, attentive.

"Guilt tells me 'I did something bad.' Shame says 'I am bad.' That's how I felt. I was incapable of right action. I was doomed. I had zero self-respect. Until," Mac paused to survey the people seated at the tables, "I found you guys, until I found a program of recovery. For me, this is a process of healing. I lived too long in a dark hole of misery and loneliness. Today, I've emerged into the light of companionship and community. And I'm forever grateful. That's all I've got."

The sharing continued until it was Hood's turn.

"I'm Francis," he said. "I think I'll just listen."

"Thanks, Francis."

"We're glad you're here."

"Keep coming back."

When the meeting ended, Hood lingered, as usual, for his one-on-one session with his recovery sponsor, Matthew.

"So, anything new to report?" Matthew asked. The two men sat perpendicular to each other at the corner of a table.

"Well, I reached out to a guy who I suspect may have a drinking problem, and he pretty much told me to mind my own business." Matthew asked for specifics, and Hood related — without naming names — his past and present history with David and Cheryl Grimm. He concluded with the episode at their house, where he escorted Cheryl to retrieve some belongings and confronted David in the kitchen.

When the sheriff finished, Matthew said, "Sounds like this thing is still bothering you."

"It's been on my mind, yeah. I can't seem to get it out of my head."

"Why not?"

"I don't know. I was hoping you could tell me."

Matthew shrugged. "For me, I don't like loose ends. I can see how you, being a law enforcement officer, like things to be solved, wrapped up. I'm guessing you find satisfaction in closing a case, so to speak. Your encounter with the husband, however, was the exact opposite."

"That makes sense."

"You reached out, Francis. You didn't have to. From what you told me, I could see how you could still harbor a big resentment against this guy. He sounds like an ass. He treated you badly, treated his wife badly. And yet you made an effort."

"Why do I feel like I didn't do enough?"

"I felt that way for a long time. Still do, to some extent. But there are limits to what I can do. I can't make you sober. I can be available if you reach out for help, but I can't force you to reach out. The longer I'm in this program, the more I realize there are lots of people who could benefit from recovery, but want no part of it."

"It's frustrating."

"All I can do is plant the seed. Sometimes it takes time, sometimes it doesn't take at all."

"So, I'm just supposed to be okay with that?"

"My sponsor once told me something. He said, 'You can't perform God's miracle. You don't have that power.' It's a humbling thought, but it's true."

"Sometimes, humility sucks."

"That's true. Sometimes, we have to be content with being an example of recovery, not a promoter."

GHOUL DUTY

* * * * *

Dusk shrouded the neighborhood as Hood turned the cruiser onto his street, approached his house, and spotted the ghostly outline of the black Chevy pickup. It was parked at the curb across the street and one house down from his own. He sped forward and was out of his vehicle in the instant the cruiser came to a complete stop.

"Schrock," he shouted into the gathering darkness. A bizarre combination of confusion, frustration, and anger coursed through his body.

He looked inside the truck's cab—empty—then scanned the sidewalks and yards.

"Schrock," he called again.

Nothing.

"I know you can hear me. Come out where—" he stopped, glimpsing motion in the periphery of his vision.

Schrock appeared from the side of a neighboring house. He stopped and stared at the sheriff.

"Look, I'm sorry about your father," Hood muttered, as much to himself as to Schrock, who remained silent as Hood approached him, "but if you've got to get back at somebody, I'm right here. Leave my family out of this." Hood felt an infusion of adrenaline as he closed to within a few feet of Schrock before his progress abruptly was halted; two massive arms had extended from behind and enclosed him in a vice-like bear hug.

Hood struggled and kicked, but the constriction only tightened, followed by the whispered words—"Don't do it, please" — from his deputy, Lester Stackhouse. Hood relaxed with the recognition that his captor was acting as his protector.

"Heath," Lester said, maintaining his hold on his boss, "get the hell out of here."

Schrock looked at Lester, then at Hood. He grinned slightly.

"Now," Lester ordered.

Lester waited until Schrock had driven away before releasing his grip. "Sorry," he said. "I didn't know what you were going to do."

"Neither did I." Hood straightened his uniform.

"I was afraid he was trying to bait you," Lester said. "You know, goad you into roughing him up, then making something of it."

Hood considered the possibility.

"I just found out," Lester continued, "Schrock's doing some yard work for your neighbor here. That's what I came to tell you. Figured you needed to know in case you saw him. He and his cousin went door-to-door looking for odd jobs, and your neighbor hired them to haul off branches, clean out a shed, stuff like that."

Hood studied his deputy.

"We okay, boss?" Lester asked. "When I saw you, I didn't know what else —"

"We're okay," Hood assured.

"Okay."

As Lester turned to leave, Hood added, "And thanks."

CHAPTER
21

When Hood heard the news about the prison assault on Buddy Monroe, he responded immediately to Huhman County Hospital and located Lisa in the third-floor waiting area, outside the surgical suites. She was seated, bent at the waist, her face hidden in her open hands, but Hood heard no sounds of weeping or crying.

He approached. "How's Buddy?"

She looked up, revealing black, blue, and yellow bruising on her right cheek and around her right eye. Swelling puffed her upper lip.

"What happened to you?" Hood blurted, surprise dictating his question.

"This," she gestured to her face, "is nothing. Buddy's fighting for his life."

"Have they told you anything?"

"The doctors or the prison?"

"Either."

"The prison official who called me just said Bud assaulted and was taken here."

Hood was encouraged that she spoke civil' apparent malice toward him. "Let me see wb out." Retreating to a hallway, he called Mark assistant warden he had worked with on prison escapes, failures to return from furloughs, and other prison-related offenses. Fennewald was unfamiliar with the assault on Buddy, but promised to review the incident and return the sheriff's call.

Hood moved to a window overlooking a courtyard and gazed at a large wire sculpture of an angel arising from a surrounding mosaic of lawns, shrubs, and paths.

"Francis?" Matthew's familiar voice interrupted Hood's musings. Hood and his recovery sponsor exchanged greetings. In answer to Matthew's implied question, Hood explained why he was at the hospital and asked, "You doing volunteer work?"

"New Opportunities," Matthew said. "You know I can't name names, Francis, but we enrolled someone in the intensive outpatient program the other day. I only mention it because he showed me your business card with our program written on the back."

Hood smiled.

"Plant the seed, Francis," Matthew said. "Well, I've got to run."

As Matthew disappeared around the corner, Hood's cell phone rang. He answered Fennewald's call immediately.

"Preliminary report says Buddy Monroe was assaulted by Kevin Jackson," the assistant warden said. "Jackson's got multiple sentences, probably never going to see the outside. From what we've been able to piece together, Jackson stabbed Buddy multiple times with a sharpened hunk of metal. Don't know where he got it yet. Jackson's in custody, and we've got the shiv."

"This Jackson guy and Buddy have history?" Hood asked.

"Zero. It doesn't even look like they knew each other, but Jackson's been known to do some dirty work for Jimmy Kronk." Hood knew Jimmy Kronk largely by the inmate's reputation as a prison power broker who rewarded or punished for a price.

"Thanks," Hood said. He disconnected, returned to the waiting room, and briefed Lisa on what he had learned. In answer to his question, she said she had never heard her husband mention Kevin Jackson or Jimmy Kronk. Nearly a half hour later, a physician wearing surgical scrubs appeared. He told Lisa and Hood that the surgery was successful and Buddy was stable. He said Buddy had suffered four stab wounds — one to the hand, obviously a defensive wound, another in the shoulder and two to the abdomen. The abdominal wounds were the most dangerous and, despite the surgery, potentially problematic. The surgeon assured them, however, that medical personnel were doing everything possible.

The soiled shovel was the only item on the immaculate stainless-steel tabletop.

Hood had called Sandra Brondel at the Highway Patrol crime lab to ask if he could come by to look at the shovel that had Haulenbach's blood and tissue on the blade and Creighorn's fingerprints on the handle.

"What are we looking for?" she asked as they stared at the implement.

"Don't know," Hood said. "At this point, I'd take any kind of break at all." He studied the shovel, positioned with the back of the blade facing them.

"That," she said, pointing to an indentation in the metal where the sleeve connected to the wooden shaft, "is where I found the samples." Hood focused on the blade, where the words "Tempered Steel" were etched on the side of the sleeve. He inspected the wooden shaft and the faded print of the manufacturer's name, HandyWorks.

Hood consulted his notebook and what he had written about the respective interviews with Herman and Creighorn. Herman didn't recall the manufacturer of the shovels in his truck; Creighorn wasn't certain, but admitted he had purchased some HandyWorks tools.

At Hood's request, Sandra pulled on sterile gloves and turned over the shovel. The sheriff scrutinized the face of the blade, as well as the remainder of the handle. He asked if she had found any other identifying marks and was told she had not.

"And this was it?" Hood said. "There was nothing else in either truck that could be linked to Haulenbach's death?"

She shook her head. Experience had taught her these types of questions typically were an indication of an officer's frustration, not mistrust of her thoroughness. "No," she answered. "We got some fiber samples from Herman's cab that are consistent with the clothing Haulenbach was wearing when you found his body, but Herman already told us Haulenbach was a passenger. There were no other traces of blood or tissue."

Hood looked up at her, his expression revealing his puzzlement.

"What?" she asked.

"I don't know. Something isn't right."

CHAPTER

22

ANFO.

The letters commanded Hood's attention.

He had been reading and organizing the backlog of paperwork that had languished on his desk since his Maryland trip. As he neared the bottom of the stack, the acronym all but shouted at him. Hood knew ANFO—ammonium nitrate/fuel oil—was a powerful explosive commonly used for excavation, construction, and earth-moving. He checked the date of the report Young John had taken while Hood was on the East Coast, then read the particulars.

ANFO and boosters for detonation were reported stolen from the warehouse at Creighorn Excavating Co. The timing of the theft was undetermined; it could have happened at any time since the explosive was last used, which was nearly a week before it was discovered missing. No signs of forced entry were found to the fenced grounds, locked main gate, or warehouse itself.

Leaving his office, Hood noticed Young John's desk was unoccupied and scanned the interior. He spotted Wally standing near a window, speaking on his cell phone.

"Okay, brother," Wally said as Hood approached. "Gotta go."

Before Hood could speak, Wally said, "That was Herman on the phone, but we were talking about Dad's birthday coming up, not the case."

"Relax," Hood said. "I don't expect you not to talk to your brother." He paused. "That's not what this is about. I was just catching up on reports. You know anything about a theft of ANFO from Creighorn's company?"

"ANFO? When?"

"Young John took the report the day I left for Maryland. It's been sitting in my inbox since then."

"First I've heard of it," Wally said.

"Okay." Hood started for the exit.

"Where you going?" Wally asked.

"To see Creighorn."

"Alone?"

Hood shrugged. "Wanna go?"

"Sure. If it's okay."

"It's okay with me. This is about a theft, not the Haulenbach case."

"It's Saturday," Wally said. "He won't be at the job site."

"I was planning to stop by his cabin. See if he's got more details."

Hood turned onto Old Sawmill Road and followed its descent into the bottomlands protected by the Clarke Junction Levee. He exited onto the lane that separated farmers' fields from dense woods, then onto the rutted drive leading to Creighorn's cabin.

"I'm not expecting trouble," Hood said to Wally, "but, just to be safe, hang back and keep an eye out." Wally nodded as his boss drove into the clearing surrounding the structure Creighorn called his "cabin." Although its exterior was constructed of rustic logs, it was a three-bedroom homestead and hunting lodge complete with a kitchen, two baths, a stone chimney, and an expansive front porch.

The humidity and heat settled on Hood the moment he exited the cruiser, and the serenity of his surroundings seemed somehow unsettling. Birds and squirrels provided the only activity; their sounds, the gentle rustle of the leaves, and the distinct hum of the cabin's air conditioner created the only noise. While Wally remained near the cruiser, the sheriff approached the cabin, climbed the porch steps, and knocked on the door. No answer. He knocked again and heard footsteps approaching from within.

The door was opened by a haggard-looking Creighorn wearing soiled jeans and an equally filthy sleeveless T-shirt. He was barefoot, his hair was disheveled, and his watery eyes and vacant stare indicated intoxication. "What the hell do you want?" he slurred.

"I'm following up on a reported theft from your company," Hood said.

Creighorn squinted, as if trying to comprehend. "Oh, that." He paused. "Well, now ain't a good time."

Hood rubbed his cheek. "I suppose we could go to the department and sit you in an interrogation room until you sober up."

"Fuck you," Creighorn said, producing a mixture of drool and spittle. He looked past Hood to where Wally stood by the cruiser. "What the fuck's he doin' here? I thought he was s'posed to stay away."

"We're just here about the theft."

"Fuck the theft. I withdraw the report. Okay?" Creighorn turned to walk back inside.

"It's not that simple," Hood said. "ANFO's dangerous. Besides, we can't ignore a crime once it's been —"

Creighorn glared at Hood. His face was reddened with rage. "Look, I'll settle this thing with the punk ex-con who flattened my tires, took my keys, and ripped off my warehouse." He inhaled a breath. "And while we're at it, I got no idea how Travis's brains got on my shovel."

"You told me you lost your keys."

"Yeah, well I lied." Creighorn yanked the key ring from his pocket, the skull fob setting off a dissonant jangle. "But I got 'em back and —"

He was halted in mid-sentence by a sudden, unexpected explosive blast that reverberated through the trees and flushed birds into frenzied flight.

Hood and Creighorn faced the source of the sound. Although they could see nothing through the stand of tall trees, they heard a low rumble gather momentum, building gradually into a roaring sound as if stampeding behemoths were breaking and crushing the forest in an approaching onslaught.

"What the —?" Hood said, stupefied by the sound.

"Levee broke," Wally shouted, as the revelation flooded his thoughts. "Head for the trees. Climb as high as you can, and hang on."

"Fuck that," Creighorn yelled. He disappeared into his cabin.

With Wally leading, Hood sprinted toward the woods. Behind him, he heard the screams of timber — limbs, saplings, entire trees — bowing and collapsing beneath the rushing weight of water. As he neared a massive oak with a low-hanging branch he could grab, Hood caught a glimpse of Wally clinging to the limbs of a nearby cottonwood. Hood leaped, seized a branch with his left hand and the crook of his right elbow, then pulled himself up. As he scrambled higher into the branches, unmindful of the rough bark rasping his skin and the limbs gouging fresh scratches on his face and arms, the massive wall of water splintered the cabin and plowed forward its logs, planks, and shingles.

Hood realized in that moment he wasn't high enough above the ground and had no time to climb higher. He hugged a large branch, flattened his body against the trunk, and braced for the impact. The water hit him like a battering ram. He swirled beneath the surface, turning involuntary somersaults as he clung to the branch, which he realized had been torn from the trunk. He needed air but — not knowing which direction led to the surface — clung desperately to the branch. His arms, legs, and torso were pummeled by debris careening all around him.

He knew he was out of air. His lungs burned for lack of oxygen. He tried to visualize that he could hold his breath still longer, but failed. He opened his lips and felt water begin to fill his mouth and seep into his throat. The branch popped to the surface, and he coughed up muddy water as he greedily sucked air through his nostrils.

As with an ocean swimmer who dives deep to avoid the pounding force of the surf, the time he had spent submerged had released him from the forward thrust of the wave of water. Already, the newest addition to the floodwaters was dispersing in search of its own level. He clutched the branch and gazed at the portions of protruding trees as floodwaters continued to carry him along, swiftly, but no longer dangerously. He felt exhilaration at having survived the ordeal, but it quickly was displaced by fears for Wally's fate. As he scanned the surface in search of his deputy, he turned and saw the massive wall of cabin logs bearing down on him like a runaway barge.

CHAPTER
23

Hood was drifting on the periphery of consciousness.

Willing himself to move, he touched off a sharp pain that radiated throughout his body. When he attempted to shape the word, "Wally," no sound came from his mouth. All he heard was a faint hum of machinery and indistinguishable traces of voices that seemed distant.

Hood is walking.

The atmosphere is a misty, gauzy gray. He walks along a muddy lane, little more than a path that parallels the river. As he walks, the landscape before him recedes at a corresponding tempo. Whether he quickens or slows his pace seems to make no difference. He glances at his feet and confirms he is moving forward, but when he looks ahead, he sees he has made no progress.

He realizes—with sudden embarrassment—he is unsure of his destination. The dense mist thickens and obscures his view, so he stops and closes his eyes. When he opens them, he sees—in the distance—a white fence with a gate. Beyond is the facade of a modest one-story house with a door in the center and a window on each side.

GHOUL DUTY

He steps forward, expecting the house to recede, but it does not. He approaches, slowly, deliberately, cautiously. Opening the gate, he walks along a stone walkway. The front door opens inward, revealing an interior room. He looks inside and sees a brick fireplace, a small table with a lamp and, on the opposite wall, a door. He steps inside. A wood fire warms the room; the table lamp lights the interior.

He closes the entry door and hears a lock click. He moves to the fire. As heat warms him, he notes the fire doesn't need to be tended, stoked, or fed additional logs. It is ideal. He crosses to the interior door and turns the knob. The door opens to a dimly lit, narrow, gray corridor. He enters and notices no apparent source of the light. He walks the length of the long hallway until he encounters another door. He twists the knob and enters another room. On the opposite wall is a second door. The room is windowless. On the wall to his left is a large chalkboard — like those found in a classroom — with a narrow tray along its bottom length. The tray contains a piece of chalk. A floor lamp illuminates the room. The board, chalk, and lamp are the only items there.

He uses the chalk to write a question mark on the board and steps back to assess his work. A second question mark appears, almost magically, on the board. The second symbol is larger and canted at an angle. As he watches, additional question marks materialize on the board. They are larger or smaller than the original and written — as if by some invisible hand — at varying angles, including upside-down. New marks continue to appear as he returns the chalk to the tray and exits the room by the second door.

The corridor he enters is reminiscent of the first, except he descends three concrete steps before walking a considerable distance, where he climbs three ascending concrete steps. He continues walking for what seems a long time before coming upon another door. He opens the door and steps inside another windowless room, again with a second door on the facing wall. Inside the room is an artist's easel holding a blank canvas. On a small table beside the easel are paints and brushes. Track lighting along the ceiling provides ample light.

He bypasses the art supplies as he crosses the room and opens the second door, which leads to yet another corridor. He proceeds, climbing two steps and, almost immediately, descending two steps before continuing to another door.

The pattern—alternating corridors and rooms—continues. One room contains only a grand piano; another features a writing desk with a typewriter and sheets of blank paper; still other rooms are outfitted for a singular purpose. As he continues through what seems an endless succession, he wonders if he has been walking in a circle. His sense of direction, however, suggests his progress has been linear; although the pattern continues, it never repeats.

He pauses in one of the elongated corridors and considers that the facade of the house, like seeing the front of a locomotive, offers no clue regarding the length of what follows. Although he hears no sounds, he listens. He listens intently, but the silence is equally intense. So intense, it triggers fear. His trepidation is slight at first, but grows exponentially.

He wonders if turning back is an option. What if he — like a pawn on a chessboard — can only move forward?

He dismisses the notion. He will not turn back. He has come too far.

Then a new fear forms. What will happen when he reaches the end? What will he find?

He knows he must choose. But he remains immobile, seemingly paralyzed.

"Francis."

The voice was faint, like a whisper diminishing down a long tunnel.

He listened and heard it again, more distinct.

"Francis."

He twitched, almost automatically, and felt a squeeze of his left hand. The pressure was warm, slightly damp.

"Francis."

He tried to focus on speaking, but his voice was unresponsive. He tensed his hand.

"Oh my God."

The voice was unmistakable.

"Oh my God," Linda repeated. "He squeezed my hand."

* * * * *

The features were indistinct but recognizable. "Linda?" Hood said, a faint croak.

"I'm here, Francis."

He tried to shake off the drug-induced stupor, but failed. He managed a one-word question. "Wally?"

"He's here in the hospital," Linda said. "Only a few doors down."

"Alive," Hood said, a joyful whisper.

"Yes," Linda said. "He'll need some rehab, but he'll be fine."

Hood was eager for details, but his mind and body craved rest. Before drifting back to sleep, he murmured another word: "Keys."

Hood is drifting again.

Floating in semi-consciousness is both comforting and frustrating. He is aware of a voice—a woman's voice. He is aware of fingers touching the backs of his hands. He does not recognize the voice or the touch; they are faint. He urges himself to focus, to break the surface into consciousness, but he cannot. At least, not at this moment.

A fleeting thought reminds him to live in the present. But, there is no present. The moment it arrives, it is gone. He tells himself he will have time later. He will take care of everything later.

GHOUL DUTY

* * * * *

Hood sat in a chair at Wally's bedside.

In the two days since regaining consciousness, he had become accustomed to the antiseptic smell that had seemed so pervasive and noxious. Now, it was barely noticeable. He instinctively reached upward, pressed his fingers against the bandana-like bandage that circled his head, and compared their respective injuries. Hood had suffered a concussion and a large gash on his forehead that required multiple stitches. Although he was restricted to walking with assistance or using a wheelchair, he was mobile.

In contrast, Wally was confined to a hospital bed, his left leg elevated by a suspended trapeze of chrome tubing, braided wires, and pulleys. Beyond the compound leg fracture, however, the deputy had suffered only minor cuts and bruises.

"Your wife stopped by to visit yesterday," Wally said. "That was thoughtful."

Hood nodded.

"If you don't mind my asking, how are you two doing?"

"She's been here a lot. Even when I was pretty much out of it, I'm told she was here almost constantly."

"That's a good sign."

"Yeah, but I don't want to rush it. I tried that at first, but I finally realized it has to be her decision. I think she might be waiting for me to get a year of sobriety. She mentioned her sister told her the first year can be tricky."

"That's coming up soon, though, right?"

"End of July—about two months."

"Good," Wally said. "Guess who else stopped by."

"No idea."

"Cheryl Grimm."

"Cheryl? Why?"

"She said she came to visit you, but you were sedated and pretty much incoherent."

Hood knew he would need to consider how to approach Cheryl, but not now. He was pleased when Wally changed the subject and asked, "Any news on Creighorn?"

"Still missing," Hood answered. "The Ghoul Duty crews have added him to the list."

"Him or his body?"

"It's been four days. I'm thinking it's a recovery operation."

"Unless he's hiding."

"From?"

"Maybe he thinks you're going to arrest him for Haulenbach's murder."

"The evidence isn't there," Hood said. "Besides, I'm having second thoughts. Did you hear what Creighorn said to me—before the explosion, I mean?"

"Bits and pieces. He sounded pretty drunk. I couldn't make out all the words from where I was standing."

"He said he didn't know how Haulenbach's brains got on his shovel."

Wally hesitated a long moment. "And you believed him?"

Hood scratched the bandage on his head in a futile attempt to relieve the itching beneath it. "Yeah, I did."

Wally's expression revealed skepticism, but he said nothing.

"I'll tell you what else Creighorn said," Hood continued. "He said he'd settle things with the 'punk ex-con' — those were his words — who took his keys and stole the ANFO from his warehouse. He had to be referring to Heath Schrock."

Wally considered the allegation. "If Schrock had Creighorn's keys, that would explain why there were no signs of forced entry in the theft at the excavating company."

"Exactly," Hood said. He realized it had been a long time since he and Wally had engaged in this type of collaboration on an investigation. He also appreciated that the give-and-take could be both therapeutic and productive. "But the question I keep coming back to is: Why destroy the levee? I mean, what's down there except woods, farmers' fields, and a few cabins?"

"Maybe Creighorn was the target," Wally said. "Maybe it was unfinished business."

"What unfinished business?"

"The bar-fight, maybe. There's bad blood between those two."

"Maybe," Hood said, his tone retaining skepticism. "Still seems like overkill."

"For a reasonable person, maybe," Wally said. "But I don't see anything in Schrock's history — or Creighorn's, for that matter — that suggests moderation."

CHAPTER
24

Hood's release from the hospital was accompanied by advice from his doctor—and from Linda—to rest comfortably. His mind, body, and soul argued otherwise. Action was the only way Hood knew to calm his raw emotions and chaotic thoughts. Among those thoughts was Creighorn's reference to having his keys stolen by an "ex-con," a reference that pointed to Heath Schrock.

He flipped through his notes and found the address Schrock had provided to his probation officer, Janelle. Hood called Lester. "I want to pay a visit to where Heath Schrock is staying with his cousin. Can you meet me at 404 Alcorn in, say, fifteen minutes?"

"Done," Lester said.

When Hood arrived, Lester already had parked his cruiser three doors down from the specified address. The two lawmen exited their vehicles, crossed the unkept lawn and approached the shabby house. Hood sensed immediately no one was home, but went through the motions of repeatedly knocking at the door and walking around the house.

"Now what?" Lester asked.

Hood considered his options and decided his next step was to question Lisa, who might have more information about the assault on her husband or the feud involving Creighorn and Schrock. He instructed Lester to resume his patrol, but to check the Alcorn address periodically.

Back in his cruiser, Hood called The Sportsmen's and was told Lisa had left to visit her husband in the hospital. He was headed there when his ring tone sounded. The display identified Mark Fennewald, the assistant prison superintendent, as the caller. Hood answered.

"Francis," Fennewald said, "I thought I'd give you an update, even though it's not much. Buddy's attacker won't talk — not a word. We've tried carrots and sticks, but he won't budge. That means somebody's got a grip on him tighter than any reward or punishment we can offer, and we figure that somebody is Jimmy Kronk."

"Great," Hood said, his sarcasm apparent. "Jimmy's a hard case."

"Agreed," Fennewald said. "We know Jimmy's a non-starter, so we put out some feelers and got a line on a guard who might be doing some trafficking, and not just dope. We've been monitoring him on the job but, so far, nothing. I thought you might want to check on how he spends his time off."

"Name?"

"Dwayne Rehagen. Lives east of the city on Woodside Court. Number 726-B."

"I know the neighborhood," Hood said. "Mostly duplexes."

"While I've got you on the phone, anything new on Buddy?"

"Haven't heard, but I'm heading to the hospital now."

"Keep me posted, okay?"

"Okay." Hood disconnected and immediately called Young John. He relayed Fennewald's information, asked Young John to stake out Rehagen's duplex and to report any activity, no matter how seemingly commonplace.

As he parked in the lot, Hood smiled at the irony of revisiting the hospital he was so glad to be discharged from only a day ago. Inside Buddy's hospital room, a Corrections officer sat near the door. Lisa stood beside her husband's bed, watching him sleep.

"How is he?" Hood asked her as he approached.

"Still stable. Not much change. They've been keeping him pretty sedated."

Hood seated himself and faced her. "Lisa, you know they've identified Buddy's assailant as Kevin Jackson."

She nodded.

"Jackson's not cooperating. We have reason to believe someone paid for a hit on Buddy. We also believe an inmate named Jimmy Kronk may have brokered the deal. What we need to know is whether Buddy ever mentioned someone who might have a reason — "

"Corrections asked me the same thing," Lisa said. "That's all I keep thinking about." She rubbed her palms together. "Who would do this? I keep replaying my conversations with Buddy over and over, but there's nothing. He never mentioned fights, arguments, nothing."

"Okay," Hood said. He remained silent, sensing Lisa had become more upset.

After a time, she asked, "Creighorn still missing?"

Hood nodded. "We're still looking."

"I'm guessing he's dead by now." After a moment, she added, "And good riddance, too."

"I know there's no love lost between you and Creighorn."

"No love lost between anybody and Creighorn. He's got a few toadies, is all."

Hood saw his opportunity and seized it. "A while back, Creighorn said someone stole his keys and punctured the tires on his truck in The Sportsmen's lot. Know anything about that?"

She shook her head. "All I know is he was plenty pissed one night when he came in to use the phone."

"Did he say anything about what happened?"

"Look, I just draw beer. What's with all these questions?"

"I'm trying to determine if Creighorn was the target of the levee explosion. Have you heard any talk about somebody wanting to get even with him?"

Lisa chuckled. "All the time."

"You know what I mean."

She shook her head, indicating no.

"Hear anything about explosives being stolen from Creighorn's company?"

"Heard it happened, just like everybody else, but no names."

Hood waited a few beats, then said, "You never told me who's responsible for those bruises on your face."

"You never asked."

"I'm asking now."

Lisa glared at him. "I think I'm tired of this conversation."

"And I'm tired of this bullshit," Hood said, his anger rising. "I've got a missing Ansel Creighorn, a chief deputy with a compound fracture, and a gash in my head, and I think you know more than you're telling me." He inhaled a long breath. "I'm tired, too. I'm tired of rain, tired of floods, tired of people dying and people withholding information. But I'm not too tired to seek a subpoena to haul you in for questioning under oath."

"You gotta be kidding me."

"You know I'm not," Hood said, his tone adamant. "One way or another, you're going to answer my questions."

Lisa twisted her expression into a combination of smirk and surrender. "What the hell," she said. "I don't know who I'm protecting or what I'm protecting him from anyway. Creighorn cut me off in traffic a while back. I think he was drunk. He knocked me around some," she said, gesturing toward her face. "Cody, too. He asked where he could find Heath, said—"

"Heath Schrock?"

"Yeah. Creighorn said if I saw Heath to tell him he was a dead man, or something like that."

"Did you—see Heath, I mean?"

"Yeah. He came by my apartment the next day. I didn't want to let him in, but he already knew what happened after talking to my son. Heath knew it was Creighorn, too, without me telling him."

"What did Heath say?"

Lisa looked away. "Said he was gonna take care of it."

"And you believed him?"

Lisa nodded.

"Did he say anything about explosives?"

"No," she said. "He never mentioned anything like that."

"You know where he is?"

She shook her head. "I think he said he's staying with a relative—a cousin or uncle or something—but I don't have the address."

"Okay," Hood said, his tone softened. "Thanks." He left the room.

For the second time that day, Hood and Lester approached the house on Alcorn. Hood had been in the hospital elevator when his deputy called and reported a car—a dull blue Chevrolet Monte Carlo, not a black pickup—now was parked in the driveway at the residence.

Hood rapped on the front door, and, when it opened, the marijuana odor wafting from the interior prompted him to step back and fan his face with his hand. Amid the haze, a man emerged onto the stoop. He appeared to be in his early thirties, wearing wrinkled, oversized shorts, a tattered T-shirt, and a glazed expression. He pulled the door closed behind him.

"I'm your sheriff, Francis Hood."

"Oh shit, man," the resident said, his voice resigned.

"Relax," Hood said. "I'm not here to bust you."

"Awright," the man muttered as he nodded his head repeatedly.

"And your name is?"

"Freddie." He wobbled slightly, as if he might topple backward.

After learning Freddie's last name and that he was the owner of the house, Hood said, "Well, Freddie, I'm looking for Heath Schrock or his cousin Ronnie."

"They're not here, man. I mean, they were, but they're not now."

"Heath listed this address as his residence."

"I dunno, man. I mean, Ronnie lived here—paid rent and stuff—and he was letting his psycho cousin stay here, but they been gone a few days and they took their stuff."

"They moved out?"

"I dunno, man. I just know they're gone and their stuff is gone. Hey, I hope you're not gonna repeat that 'psycho' remark 'cause that Heath guy is not cool, man."

"Don't worry," Hood said. "Mind if we come in and look around?"

The question seemed to sober Freddie somewhat. "I don't know, man. The place is kind of a mess."

"Freddie, this isn't an inspection, and I'm not interested in your stash. If I was going to bust you, you'd be handcuffed in the back of the patrol car by now."

"So why do you wanna look around?"

"See if Ronnie or Heath left anything behind that might help me find them."

Freddie looked down at his unlaced sneakers. "As long as those guys don't find out, I guess —"

The ringing of Hood's cell phone interrupted.

The caller, Young John, said, "Schrock just showed up on the prison guard's porch."

"I'm on my way," Hood said.

"Shit," Young John's disembodied voice said. "He spotted me."

"See if —"

"He's on the run," Young John said.

As he drove to Dwayne Rehagen's address, Hood was not surprised by the follow-up call from Young John, who reported Schrock had outrun and eluded him. He instructed his deputy to remain at the scene and detain Rehagen if he tried to leave. Hood arrived within minutes. "Dwayne Rehagen," he said to the man who stood beside Young John on the porch of the duplex. "I'm your sheriff, Francis Hood."

"What's going on?"

"My deputy spotted a person we're interested in, Heath Schrock, at your front door."

"Heath who?"

"Schrock."

Rehagen shook his head. "Don't know any Schrock."

"We'd like to know what his business is with you."

"Look, some guy just showed up at my door. I don't know if he was selling something or what, but when I opened the door, he ran off."

"Not what I saw," Young John interjected. "You and Schrock had a conversation, and you motioned for him to come in. That's when he turned around, saw me, and took off."

"Okay," Rehagen said. "He's an ex-con who just got out—wanted to borrow some money."

"I don't think so," Hood countered. "I think he wanted an explanation."

"About what?"

"About why Buddy Monroe is still breathing. About how the hit you helped arrange between Heath Schrock and Jimmy Kronk got botched."

"You're crazy."

"And you're in a bad spot between those two, and they're both pissed off right now. Think this through for a minute," Hood said. "Heath paid for something he didn't get, he knows where you live, he came to your house, and he spotted a sheriff's cruiser. I'll bet he's thinking you're gonna rat him out."

Hood watched Rehagen's expression transform from smug confidence to abject fear. "I got nothin' to worry about," he muttered, without conviction.

"Just keep telling yourself that," Hood said. "But if you want to talk to the authorities about exchanging information for protection, you know where to find me."

CHAPTER
25

An array of rakes, hoes, shovels, and pitchforks hung on sheets of pegboard lining a wall at Bunch Farm and Home Supply, owned and operated by Young John's father Andrew Bunch. Gardening never had been among Hood's hobbies. He dutifully mowed and trimmed his lawn, but unlike some of his neighbors, he derived no pleasure or pride from imposing immaculate order by vanquishing weeds, pruning greenery, or nurturing flowers.

The implements were arranged on the wall by type, not by manufacturer. He located shovels made by HandyWorks and removed two models that, based on his recollection, looked most like the shovel he had examined at the crime lab. The heft of the tool and its balance felt comfortable. He could almost feel its potential power being transmitted to his hands. He wondered briefly about man's attraction to tools throughout history, about how they could be used for both construction and destruction. Hood realized he was being distracted by his own thoughts and scolded himself. He refocused on the shovels, which seemed similar but not identical to the tool seized from Creighorn's truck.

Taking out his cell phone, he called Sandra Brondel's

number at the crime lab. After exchanging greetings, he said, "I'm at the Farm and Home looking at shovels."

"Okay?" she said, her questioning tone apparent.

"Can you do me a favor?"

"Sure."

"Can you get on your computer and see if any of the shovels made by HandyWorks match our murder weapon?"

Hood could almost hear her puzzling over his request during the silence before she asked, "What are you thinking?"

"I'm thinking something's not right."

Hours later, Hood was at his office, focused on his daily duties when his cell phone sounded, signaling he had received a text. A message from Sandra read: "At the lab. May have found something."

"On my way," he replied.

Although she was expecting him, her gasp when he entered the lab indicated she wasn't expecting the row of stitches across his forehead. "My God," she said, holding her fingertips over her mouth. "I heard about the concussion, but—"

"It looks worse than it is," Hood said. "Now what's this about finding something?"

"Over here," she said, as she led him to her desk and directed him to the computer screen. She clicked the mouse, and the monitor displayed two rows of images of shovels.

"These are the types of shovels manufactured by HandyWorks," she said. "Now this," she continued as she clicked and displayed a single image of a shovel, "is our suspected murder weapon. I scaled down the photo to match the proportions of the others."

She looked at him. "Now watch," she said. One by one, she superimposed the suspect weapon over the other tools. None matched.

Hood thought a moment. "What about other models? You know, discontinued lines."

"I considered that, too," Sandra said, "so I called the company. It's headquartered on the West Coast, so it hadn't closed yet. I spoke with a representative of the design department. I've got his name and number if you want to call him. He said there are no discontinued models. Every shovel they manufacture is on the website."

Hood stared at her, pondering the information.

"What's more," she said. "He was intrigued by my call and asked me to email my photograph of the shovel. So I did, and guess what?"

"What?" Hood asked, both confused and impatient.

"He called me back. He said the company would never manufacture a shovel like that. He said the handle is too long for the size of the blade. He said the handle would snap easily with the amount of torque that would be created if the blade got under a root or large rock."

Hood cupped his right elbow in his left palm and pressed a finger to his lips. "If that's the case," he said, thinking aloud, "the only explanation is someone switched the handle."

"Or the blade," she added, indicating she already had thought of the possibility.

"Right," Hood agreed. "But not Creighorn. He wouldn't attach a blade with incriminating evidence to a handle with his fingerprints."

"Which points to one or both of the other two people we know were out there—Herman and Neil," Sandra said.

"Or Heath Schrock," Hood added.

"Heath Schrock? But did he even know those three guys before he went to prison? Besides, he was incarcerated when Travis Haulenbach was killed. Are you thinking he was out on a furlough or work release in the spring?"

"I hadn't thought of that, but I'll check," Hood said. "Actually, I was thinking maybe he tampered with evidence after he was released but before we seized the trucks from Herman and Creighorn."

"How would he even know about the shovel?"

"I don't know."

"And why would Schrock want to frame Creighorn?

"That I do know. There's some bad blood between those two," Hood said. "And I think Schrock did more than frame Creighorn. I think he stole explosives from Creighorn's company and blew up the levee."

"Thanks for making time for me on such short notice," Hood said. He seated himself across the desk from Mark Fennewald, the assistant prison superintendent.

"Of course," Fennewald said. "I got your message about Heath Schrock's records. I checked. No furloughs, work releases, halfway house assignments, nothing. He never left the institution until the day he was released."

"Damn. I was hoping Sandra had given us a good lead to follow."

"You could've called and saved yourself the trip."

"There's one other thing." Hood described the sighting of Schrock at Dwayne Rehagen's duplex, adding that Schrock fled when he spotted Hood's deputy.

"Rehagen tried to play dumb," Hood said, "but I told him I suspected he helped Schrock set up a hit on Buddy. I also told him Schrock was upset about the botched deal and—because he saw a deputy staking out his place—Schrock would conclude Rehagen was ready to cut his losses and sell him out."

"That's harsh," Fennewald said.

Hood shrugged. "It is if I'm wrong, but the point is Rehagen's scared and he's trying to figure out his next move. I was hoping you could put on a little more pressure from your end."

"You think he'll talk?"

"If he's smart."

"I've only had a couple conversations with him," Fennewald said, "but he doesn't strike me as smart."

"I just hope he's smart enough to cop a plea to being the errand boy in a murder for hire that could put Schrock back behind bars."

"Even if you're right about Schrock arranging the hit, how much can you prove?"

"All of it, if Rehagen comes clean," Hood said. "Otherwise, my scenario makes sense, but it's not evidence. The word is Schrock has been trying to put the moves on Buddy's wife. Lisa can be a firecracker, but she's not a tramp. She's devoted to Buddy and her son. My guess is Schrock didn't like being rebuffed and thought maybe he could change the game if Buddy was out of the picture."

Fennewald rocked slightly backward in his desk chair. "Have you mentioned your theory to Buddy's wife?"

"No," Hood said.

Fennewald remained silent for a moment. "Okay," he said. "We're not sure what Rehagen's up to, but he's up to something. Let's see what we can do."

"Thanks," Hood said.

Hood pushed Wally, seated in his wheelchair, into the hospital's Contemplation Garden, a courtyard with a circular path cut through a lush lawn and featuring showy flower beds, statuary, and wooden benches. Although Hood had warned his deputy that the heat and humidity had united in another oppressive afternoon, Wally was eager to escape the confines of his hospital room. After parking him beside an unoccupied bench, Hood sat and fanned himself with his hat.

"I can't wait to get out of here," Wally said. He focused on a life-sized angel shaped from spiraled wire.

Hood nodded.

"You seem distracted," Wally said.

"I can't decide if things are coming together or falling apart."

"I take it no one's found Creighorn yet?"

"Nope. There's something else. We've got reason to believe Creighorn didn't kill Travis Haulenbach."

"I thought the shovel cinched it."

"It's not the original tool. The shovel handle and the blade don't match. The crime lab confirmed it. Apparently, someone joined those two parts from separate tools to implicate Creighorn."

"Someone put Creighorn's shovel handle on the blade that killed Haulenbach?"

"Exactly."

"But my brother and Neil were the only other people there," Wally said.

"Yes, when the murder happened, but the switch may have been made later. Weeks went by before we found Haulenbach's body and seized the trucks and tools."

"You suspect someone else?"

Again, Hood nodded. "I think Schrock may have made the switch to get back at Creighorn."

Wally considered the possibility. "But how did Schrock know to do that? And how did he get the blade with Haulenbach's blood and tissue on it?"

"That's the question I keep asking myself. I don't know. I have no idea where the shovel was from the time Haulenbach was killed until the blade turned up attached to a handle with Creighorn's prints."

"What about Neil? Have you talked to him?"

"No. Two of the other task force members interviewed him."

"You don't sound okay with that."

"I'm trying to be a team player, but I don't have a feeling for where Neil fits into this. I'd sure like to talk to him myself."

Silence ensued as each man, as if invited by the garden's purpose, engaged in quiet contemplation.

"This evidence about the shovel," Wally said, nearly a whisper. "I guess that puts my brother back in the picture as a suspect."

Hood shrugged. "I guess we can't rule anything out, but that would mean he started all this by framing himself." He looked from the sculpture to his chief deputy. "You don't have to answer, but I've got to ask: Do you think Herman could've killed Haulenbach?"

Wally refocused on the wire angel. "I want to say no. I mean, I don't think he could do it deliberately. But I've seen too many wrecks, fights, and other violence that results when people drink too much. They don't mean to hurt or kill somebody, but it happens."

"Hello, Mark," Hood said, answering the call from the assistant prison superintendent.

"Francis," Fennewald said, "I wanted to let you know Rehagen is talking."

"What's he saying?"

"Mostly what you predicted. He fingered Schrock, but not Jimmy Kronk. Rehagen said he carried an envelope from Schrock directly to Jackson. Claims he doesn't know what the message was."

"Figures. What do you think?"

"I think it's a half-truth."

"I agree."

"But I'm inclined to take it," Fennewald said. "We get Schrock back in prison, and I get rid of a bad guard. Kronk gets a pass, but he's in for the long haul anyway. What do you think?"

"It's your call, but I agree. I don't think we could do any better."

"Me neither."

"I'll pick up Schrock if I can find him. I've got my deputies looking for him but, so far, nothing."

"Tell them to be careful. If he knows we've got him connected to an attempted murder, well, I don't need to tell you."

"Thanks. Talk to you later."

The sound of the doorbell roused Hood from the semi-consciousness that precedes sleep. He arose and tied on his robe. He considered taking his sidearm, but decided a threat wouldn't be announced by ringing the doorbell. He went downstairs and looked through a front window. Cheryl stood on his front porch, illuminated by the outdoor light. She seemed composed, with no hint of panic.

Hood opened the door and stepped outside. "Are you okay?" he asked.

"I'm fine. Were you asleep?"

"No. Not yet. What's up?"

"I just wanted to talk to you."

"It's late." Hood surveyed the quiet neighborhood, illuminated only by scattered street lamps and squares of light from windows where activity continued indoors.

"Can I come in?"

"I don't think that's a good idea, Cheryl."

Silence ensued for several beats before Cheryl asked, "Worried the neighbors will see us?"

"I'm worried about what's appropriate. We're both married and we're both separated right now. This doesn't just appear wrong. It is wrong."

"Is that what you think—that this is some kind of seduction?"

"I don't know what I think. When you reappeared in my life after so many years, it brought back all kinds of memories, feelings, and emotions. I'm still trying to sort them out, but I do know that was then and this is now. And I know this," he added, extending his arms as widely as possible, "whatever this is—has to stop."

"So, your answer is no."

Hood nodded.

"I'm lost, Francis."—a whispered plea. "I don't know what to do. I just want to talk to someone."

"I'm sorry, Cheryl. I'm not the person to be talking to. I'm still trying to get my own life straightened out. I messed up my marriage—I realize that now—but I have no intention, or desire, to make things worse."

Silence followed until Cheryl said, "I guess I'd better leave."

"It's for the best."

CHAPTER
26

Hood entered A-One Auto Parts, located in the southern quadrant of Huhman County and operated by Tony Volmert. One patron sat on a stool watching Tony, who stood on the other side of the counter, searching a computer screen, presumably for a part number. "Be right with you," Tony said, without taking his eyes from the screen. He glanced up, recognized Hood and added, "Oh, hi Sheriff."

"Hello."

"What can I do for you?"

"No rush. Finish what you're doing first."

"We're just price-checking shocks. What do you need?"

"Is Neil Bowden working today?"

"Yeah. He's in the back unboxing a shipment of brake parts."

"Can I talk to him for a few minutes?"

"Sure. Go on back. Right down this aisle." Tony pointed directly behind him. "Tell him I said he can take a break—a break from the brakes, a brake break, get it?"

"Good one, Tony," the patron snickered.

Hood walked behind the counter and into the claustrophobic aisle, lined on both sides by auto parts stacked on shelving units that nearly reached the ceiling. He continued to an area where a garage door opened to a loading dock. In the center were two pallets of cardboard boxes stacked about waist high. Neil hunched over one of the cartons and severed the tape along its seam with a box cutter. His sidelong glance indicated he noticed Hood, but he returned immediately to his task.

"Need to talk to you for a few minutes," Hood said.

"I'm working."

"Tony said you could take a break."

"Don't want to spend my break talking to you. Already told you guys I didn't see nothing and I don't know nothing."

"Your pal Ansel Creighorn and Travis Haulenbach knew each other growing up in Maryland."

"So? People know people. No crime in that."

"Did Travis ever mention why he came out here? Was it to see Creighorn?"

"Never said." Neil shrugged. "All I know is Travis came to The Sportsmen's one night and Creighorn introduced him to me and Herman."

"Did Creighorn tell you how he knew Travis?"

"Not in so many words, but I could tell from their conversation they knew each other from school back in Maryland."

"What else?"

"Don't know nothing else, except it didn't take Travis long to start hitting us up for money."

"Who's us?"

"All three of us—me, Creighorn, Herman. That's when

Herman brought up the job. He told Travis he might be able to arrange for him to come work with him out at the cemetery." Neil cut open another carton and began to stack brake shoes and rotors on a cart.

"What about the levee explosion? What do you know about that?"

"Nothing. Why should I?"

"You think it had anything to do with the feud between Creighorn and Heath Schrock?"

"All I know is I was at The Sportsmen's the night they got in a fight that ended with the shotgun blast, but I didn't even know who Schrock was back then."

"There was a second incident in The Sportsmen's parking lot where I've been told Schrock flattened Creighorn's tires and took his keys."

"Heard it happened. That's about it."

Hood noticed the beginning of a tremor started in Neil's fingers, causing the box cutter he held to shake.

"But you don't know anything else about it?"

"Man, you don't quit," Neil said. "All right, look, Herman asked me not to say anything, but I saw him put Creighorn's keys on the pool table rail. Said he got the keys from Schrock."

The disclosure hit Hood like a staggering jab to the jaw, and he immediately tried to hide his reaction. "You saw Herman put Creighorn's keys on the pool table?"

"Yeah."

"And you're sure they were Creighorn's?"

"Had the skull fob and everything. Besides, Herman asked me not to say anything to Creighorn, said it would just raise a bunch of questions Herman didn't want to deal with right then."

"When was that?"

"A week or so ago. Maybe two."

"Tell me exactly what you remember."

"Me and Creighorn were throwing darts at The Sportsmen's. I went to take a leak, and when I came out, I spotted Herman in the poolroom, by himself. I went in to say 'hi' and saw him put something on the pool rail."

"Let me make sure I've got this straight," Hood said, his tone demanding certainty. "The keys Schrock took from Ansel ended up in Herman's possession — at least for some period of time — before you witnessed him put them on the pool table?"

"Yeah. Why? What's the big deal?"

Hood left the storeroom without answering. His priorities had changed. He still wanted to find Schrock, but he needed to find Herman.

A long shadow extended across the open grave — the first to be excavated in what would become the new Our Lady of Help Parish Cemetery. Herman anchored two brass rails — flanking the long sides of the rectangular hole — that would hold the straps used to lower the casket for the next day's reburial. He used a shovel to tamp the mound of soil he would cover with green, outdoor carpeting during the interment. When the hearse arrived, flowers from the funeral service at Fredrickson's Mortuary would adorn the mound. Herman stretched to his full height and saw a second elongated shadow move across the grave. He jerked his head around and faced the malevolent gaze of Heath Schrock.

"Heath," Herman said, his surprise apparent.

"You set me up," Schrock said. His tone was laced with anger and accusation.

"What're you talking about?"

"You set me up as the guy who blew up the levee. The sheriff's trying to hang that on me."

"I don't know nothing about that," Herman said. He looked around, hoping to see a fellow church employee he could summon to interrupt the confrontation. The road that led from church to cemetery cut though a stand of trees that allowed only glimpses of the building to be seen through the foliage. In addition, Herman knew he was working after hours on a day when other church personnel were unlikely to stay late. In the absence of a distraction or escape route, Herman understood his options were limited. In his most reasoned voice, he said: "Hood's just guessing about the explosion because you and Creighorn have history."

"I don't think so," Schrock said. "I gave you Creighorn's keys to return to him, but now I figure while you had them, you used them to get in, steal the explosives, and blow up the levee. And you worked it to point the finger at me."

"You got it all wrong, Heath."

"Do I. As far as—"

Herman swung the shovel. Although Schrock's reflexes were quick and he turned away and attempted to block the blow with an upraised arm, the blade caught the side of his cheek and spun him around. Before he could recover, a second blow to the temple drove Schrock to one knee. A final strike sent him sprawling into the dirt.

Hood heard the mechanical hum of the front-end loader as he came around the corner of the church. Dusk was preparing to settle as he walked along the road that led beyond the copse of trees shielding the church from its new cemetery. As Hood emerged into the expanse, he spotted Herman at the controls of the earthmover, outfitted with a bucket about the width of an open grave.

Because Herman had his back to Hood, he didn't notice the sheriff's approach. He was intent on operating the claw and scooping earth from the hole. Herman worked diligently, removing and lifting soil, then dumping it in heaps, spraying remnants of dirt and rock across the brass rails and roll of green carpeting beside the mound. Hood was baffled by the seemingly sloppy work being performed by Herman. Daylight was waning, but Herman's efforts seemed needlessly careless and hasty.

As Hood stepped nearer, the scene unfolded, revealing a sight the sheriff had not expected. Sitting on the ground, with his back propped against a tire of Herman's pickup truck,

Heath Schrock squirmed and struggled to loosen ropes binding both his arms and legs. A muddy rag was stuffed in Schrock's mouth, and his eyes were wide with fear and warning.

Confusion flooded Hood's thoughts. What, he wondered, was happening? He signaled for Schrock to be still and not acknowledge the sheriff's presence. Unholstering his sidearm, a 40-caliber Glock, Hood closed the distance between himself and Herman, who abruptly switched off the front-end loader and stood atop the machine. The sudden silence prompted Hood to sidle behind the earthmover, hidden from Herman's line of sight.

"End of the line, Heath," Herman called from atop the machine. "You were supposed to get arrested and go back to prison. Now, you'll have to disappear the same way Travis disappeared. That grave's now a couple feet deeper than normal," Herman continued as he climbed down from the earthmover. "Once your body is in that hole, I'm gonna cover it with a few feet of dirt. Our first reburial is tomorrow." He jumped to the ground. "They'll lower the casket on top of you, I'll fill in the hole, and that'll be that."

Herman stooped, picked up a shovel and approached Schrock. "Hope you'll stay put—not like Travis. I didn't really mean to kill him. Just happened, so I had to make him disappear."

Hood abruptly stepped from behind the machine, attracting Schrock's gaze, which prompted Herman to look, too.

"Sheriff," Herman said, surprised by his visitor and the gun pointed at his chest. "How long you been standing there?"

"Long enough. Put down the shovel and get on the ground," Hood ordered. "On your stomach, legs apart, hands behind your back."

"You got it all wrong," Herman said. "You got here just in time. I got Schrock — got him tied up." He gestured toward his captive. "I was just about to call you and my brother."

"On the ground," Hood repeated.

"No, look. I don't know what you heard, but I was just trying to scare him."

"I'm not going to tell you again, Herman. Put down the shovel, and get on the ground."

"I don't think so," Herman said. "You won't shoot me." He straightened to his full height, as if inflated with sudden bravado. "You wouldn't shoot your deputy's kid brother."

Hood holstered his weapon. "You're right."

He advanced toward Herman, who crouched into a defensive posture, clenching the shovel like a weapon. Hood feinted as if preparing to lunge, and Herman swung. In the instant Herman tried to recover and resume his stance, Hood delivered a powerful body block with his shoulder that propelled Herman backward. He teetered momentarily on the edge of the open grave, waving the shovel wildly in an attempt to regain his balance before tumbling into the hole.

CHAPTER
27

Hood called Maggie and requested assistance—and a ladder. Walking around the open grave, he watched Herman jump and claw frantically in a futile attempt to escape the pit.

After several minutes of flailing and cursing, Herman stood still and looked up at Hood. "You just gonna leave me here?"

"For a while," Hood answered. Then, unable to resist, he added, "Looks like you dug your own grave there."

Herman grabbed a clod of soil and flung it at the sheriff.

Hood dodged it easily, then approached Schrock, knelt beside him, and removed the rag from his mouth. Schrock spit repeatedly, leaving muddy spittle dangling from his chin. "Herman was gonna kill me and bury me in that hole," he said.

"I heard," Hood said.

"Said he'd done it before."

"Heard that, too."

"Good thing you showed up when you did. Saved my life."

Hood said nothing.

"You gonna untie me?" Schrock asked.

"No," Hood said. "I'm going to arrest you."

"For what?"

"The attempted murder of Buddy Monroe."

"You're joking."

"I'm not. We have a sworn statement. What I want you to think about is how you can help yourself by giving up Jimmy Kronk."

"No chance."

Hood heard the approaching sirens. You think about it," he said. "You're going back to prison either way. You help us, we can stash you somewhere far away from Jimmy."

"Ain't no place far enough."

Hood arose. "Not that it matters now, but I'm curious. Did you turn that propane tank loose in the river?"

Sirens blared as the first cruiser emerged into the open area of the cemetery and skidded to a halt. The alternating red and blue strobe effect from the light bar on the cruiser's roof illuminated both the dusky sky and Schrock's enigmatic grin.

"Looks like it's time," Hood said to Schrock. "Tick tock, Heath."

Hood stood in the hospital corridor outside Buddy Monroe's room and watched Lisa emerge from the elevator. She approached, carrying a tray with cafeteria food.

"How's Buddy?" he asked.

"Doctor says he's gonna be okay."

"Good." Hood looked beyond the window to the lighted Contemplation Garden. Only the top of the wire angel—its halo and the tips of its wings—was visible. He recalled what Schrock's teacher had written about his "reverence" for women, and Hood wondered whether Lisa inadvertently may have diluted or distracted Schrock from whatever vendetta he had planned for the sheriff. "I can't stay," Hood said. "I just wanted to let you know I arrested Heath Schrock for the attempted murder of your husband."

She looked at him, her expression somber and stoic. "I should be surprised, but I'm not. After Buddy was assaulted, I knew Heath was involved somehow. I didn't want to admit it, but I knew." She turned her head and tracked his focus beyond the window. "I've sat in his room for hours and hours asking myself the same question: 'Why didn't I see it coming? Why wasn't—'" She stopped in mid-sentence, overcome by her own sudden sobbing.

"Buddy and Heath will never cross paths again," Hood said, attempting to offer some consolation. "I'll see to it."

Hood smiled at his daughter as she attempted to squirm into a more comfortable position on the wooden pew in the First Christian Church sanctuary. He looked ahead to the chancel, adjacent to the altar, where his wife, Linda, was seated among other choir members. Hood turned to Elizabeth. "I know this whole separation thing has been—" he whispered.

"It's okay," his daughter said, her tone sincere.

"I don't want you to blame yourself in any way. This is all on me. I—"

"I'm just glad you're doing something about it. Aunt Sarah said it can be hard to quit. But she did it, so I know you can, too. You're my dad."

Hood buckled under the weight of her words—a vote of confidence coupled with a realistic appraisal of the challenge ahead. He turned to the chancel and attempted to make eye contact with Linda. He wanted her to know where he and Elizabeth were seated, but the first notes of the piano—the prelude to the cantata performance—prevented him from further attention-getting behavior.

Hood settled in to sounds—the phrasings of the church orchestra, the rise and fall of the choir voices, the flowing lyricism of the soloists, including Linda. When she stepped from the other robed singers and approached the microphone, he felt as if her ascending notes were lifting his spirits. When she finished, he mentally scolded himself for taking her for granted, for failing to acknowledge and appreciate her many gifts.

All too soon, the performance ended, light flooded the sanctuary, and congregants and guests milled about, greeting each other. In time, Hood, Elizabeth, and Linda found each other in a side aisle. Hood praised Linda's performance and she thanked him for attending. He hoped his compliments sounded more than obligatory. Honesty—a fundamental of his recovery program—had been much on his mind, lately. He knew Linda's appreciation was sincere; she was guileless.

But he wanted her to know his comments were an equally honest expression, stemming from a previously untapped resource within him.

In the momentary silence that followed, Elizabeth spotted her friend Claire in the center aisle and said, "I need to talk to Claire." She left, navigating her way between two pews.

Hood and his wife made their way through the diminishing crowd and into a hallway.

"What's next?" he asked. "Is there a reception? Are you sticking around?"

"No. I'm exhausted. I'm going to get out of this choir robe, grab my purse, find our daughter, and head out."

"Okay," Hood said. He smiled. "Look, I know I've been—"

Linda put a finger to her husband's lips to silence him. "Not now," she said.

"Too soon?"

She nodded. "Too soon."

Hood wanted to remind her he would be celebrating one year of sobriety in about six weeks, but didn't. He knew his motivation was to pressure Linda into offering hope they might reunite then. Instead, he said, "I know this will take time. I know I can't just expect you to trust me if I say things will be different. I just want you to know I'm starting to feel different. And I have a lot of people to thank for that—you particularly."

"You have no idea how much I appreciate that."

* * * * *

GHOUL DUTY

The floodwaters were receding, leaving the bottomlands layered with sodden silt pocked by pools and puddles awash with floating debris and withering vegetation. As the river ebbed back within its normal confines and revealed the remaining corpses, Hood stepped up his department's Ghoul Duty shifts. Only three bodies remained to be recovered — two from the Our Lady of Help Parish Cemetery and one, Ansel Creighorn, from the levee explosion. Hood sat in the bow of the johnboat, basking in the late afternoon sunlight that shimmered on the water's surface. Wally, who had been cleared to return to work, guided the craft slowly upstream.

"I visited my brother this morning," he said.

"How's Herman doing?"

"As well as can be expected, I guess."

Hood shifted in his seat so he could face his deputy. "For what it's worth, I think he and his lawyer are working out the best deal they can."

Wally nodded. "Sounds like they're willing to plead to second-degree murder for killing Travis and breaking and entering on the ANFO theft. They're still negotiating on the levee explosion and what to do about Creighorn." Wally paused. "Could be another murder charge, particularly if we find his body."

"I know Herman's facing a lot of time," Hood said, "but he caused a lot of mayhem."

"I understand that," Wally said. "But I can't help thinking how different it might be if he had just admitted from the start that he assaulted Travis but didn't mean to kill him."

Hood turned in his seat and faced forward. He considered how the incident at the parish cemetery, like his own drinking, had begun innocently enough. But as the consequences mounted, the more he tried to manage them, the worse they became. In his confession, Herman admitted he was in a drunken stupor when he attacked Haulenbach. Abandoned by his cronies and left alone with the corpse, Herman concocted the burial plan to cover up the crime. He confessed he was somewhat surprised when his false explanation of Haulenbach's disappearance was accepted — until the flood unearthed the body, which was retrieved and identified. Once that happened, Herman compounded the cover-up with another scheme. He created the counterfeit shovel before telling his fabricated blackout story to the sheriff, knowing the fingerprint evidence would shift suspicion from himself to Creighorn. As time passed, however, Herman became more paranoid that Creighorn would realize he was being framed. Herman seized a new opportunity when Schrock gave him the key ring to return to Creighorn. He used the keys to steal the ANFO and destroy the levee, knowing the evidence connected to the theft would point to Schrock.

When Wally spoke again, he shattered what had been a long silence. "My brother asked me if I could forgive him."

"Can you?" Hood asked.

"Yeah," Wally said. "You know what's tearing him up worst of all? He nearly killed me and you. He swears he didn't know we were going to be at Creighorn's cabin."

Hood remained silent.

"Remember," Wally continued, "I was on the phone with my brother that day. I told him my shift was over and I was going home. Then I ran into you, and you said it would be okay if I tagged along."

"I remember," Hood said, his tone subdued. "It's all just pretty sad."

The two men drifted into silence as their shift on the river neared its end. Wally piloted the johnboat along the south bank on the way back to the launching point.

"What's that?" Wally said, shattering the stillness and startling Hood from his reverie.

The sheriff again twisted in his seat. "Where?"

"There," Wally said. He pointed a finger. "In that debris over there."

Hood looked to the area Wally had indicated.

"Is it one?" Wally asked.

"Can't tell from here," Hood said. "Better take a look."

Wally steered the boat in a gentle arc and swept across the current toward a heap of branches and junk clustered near the riverbank. As they approached the mass, Hood hunched forward and focused on what appeared to be a body trapped among limbs and partially submerged in the water. He rubbed his neck in an effort to relieve the tension that had crept between his shoulders. Wally decelerated and leaned forward as the boat inched past a saturated pillow and sodden jacket that combined to resemble a human torso.

"False alarm," Wally said. He settled back in his seat and accelerated upstream. "Let's go home."

Hood squinted into the glare of the setting sun. He didn't protest. He was eager to move forward.

THE END

Acknowledgements

For as long as I can remember, I have valued reading and writing as opportunities to learn and grow.

My wife Kristie and adult daughters Heather and Jane are avid readers who encourage my passion to write. I am grateful for their love and support.

The image of the solitary writer tapping at a keyboard, however, reveals only a fragment of the process.

My Cave Hollow Press editors—G.B. Crump, R.M. Kinder, and Jim Taylor—opened the door for me as a novelist when they accepted my first book, *Sense of Grace*, published in the summer of 2020. They improved that manuscript and this one with their sharp editing, keen insights, and helpful suggestions.

My stories combine experience and imagination, but often require expertise I do not possess. My thanks to friends in the professional community who graciously answered my questions relating to medical, mental health, law enforcement, and judicial issues. They include former Cole County sheriffs Greg White and John Hemeyer; Michael Van Gundy, MS, licensed professional counselor; Greg Markway, Ph.D., psychologist; and Mark Schreiber, retired deputy warden, Missouri Department of Corrections. Any factual or procedural errors are mine.

I also am indebted to people who read early drafts of my work and offered suggestions. In addition to my wife, they include Phil Baker, Madeleine Leroux, and Rebecca Martin. And thanks to my "other" family for sharing their experience and encouragement.

Finally, I cannot overstate the importance of readers, book clubs, librarians, book-sellers, and others who promote authors.

About the Author

Richard F. McGonegal's debut mystery novel, *Sense of Grace*, was published by Cave Hollow Press in June 2020. *The Forget-Me-Knot*, a proposed third book in the Sheriff Francis Hood series, received the second runner-up honor at the 2021 Killer Nashville Claymore Awards for unpublished manuscripts.

In addition, 24 of his short stories have been published, including nine in *Alfred Hitchcock's Mystery Magazine*. Four of those nine have been reprinted in anthologies. He is an active member of Mystery Writers of America.

McGonegal retired in 2017 as an editor for the News Tribune Co. in Jefferson City, Mo., where he worked for more than 40 years.

He received a Bachelor of Arts degree in 1969 from Rutgers University, New Brunswick, N.J., and a Master of Arts degree in 1973 from the University of Virginia, Charlottesville. Both degrees are in English literature and language.

He and his wife, Kristie, live in Jefferson City and are the parents of two adult daughters.